CEASELESS
BOOK THREE IN THE
EXISTENCE TRILOGY

ABBI GLINES

To my soul. I hope you had the blessings and joy you've experienced in this lifetime in my past lives. If only I could remember them.

OTHER TITLES BY ABBI GLINES

In publication order by series

The Existence Series
Existence
Predestined
Leif
Ceaseless

The Rosemary Beach Series
Fallen Too Far
Never Too Far
Forever Too Far
Twisted Perfection
Simple Perfection
Take a Chance
Rush Too Far
One More Chance
You Were Mine
Kiro's Emily

The Sea Breeze Series
Breathe
Because of Low

PROLOGUE

"The soul has been marked since birth. It wasn't meant to live out this lifetime." - The Deity

"Fly away please. Stay out of my room. I could've been naked!" (Pagan -Existence)

"The soul has been appointed not once, but twice now." - The Deity

"A soul came into my house. She touched me and talked to me. Souls never talked to me, before you." (Pagan -Existence)

"If you are determined for this soul to remain by your side, then a choice must be made." - The Deity

"You can't scare me off and I'm not running away." (Pagan -Existence)

"You know that the soul has a mate. If her soul is to exist for an eternity, then the soul must choose you over the mate created as its other half." - The Deity

"This is the most precious perfect gift anyone has ever received. You gave me back a memory that I will cherish forever." (Pagan -Predestined)

"The soul has seen too much. She knows more than a soul should know. She can't keep her memories. The choice will be an unfair one if she does." - The Deity

"I'm saving it for my smoking hot boyfriend." (Pagan -Predestined)

"Every moment she has spent with you will be taken from her memories. She won't remember meeting Death and your breaking the rules to save her. She won't remember fighting for you. She won't remember the curse she suffered while under the spell of the voodoo spirit. It will all be washed clean.

If you want her, Dankmar, then you have to win her heart from the soul made to be her mate. Only then will it be possible for you to keep her for eternity.

She must pass this test." - The Deity

"Trust me, Dank Walker I will only have eyes for you. No one else even comes close." (Pagan -Predestined)

CHAPTER 1

Pagan

Miranda pulled her shiny new silver Land Rover into an empty parking spot in front of Jemison Hall, our home for the next nine months.

"Can you believe we're here?" Miranda whispered in awe as we stared up at the historic brick building in front of us. My mom was a Boone University alumna. Boone was a small private college in Weston, Tennessee. When Miranda and I had both been accepted there, I figured this was where I was meant to be. Going to a larger state university terrified me. I liked the smaller, more intimate feeling of this place.

"I'm still trying to grasp the fact that we're in college," I replied as I opened the car door.

"I know, right?"

We both stepped out of the SUV and headed for the rear cargo compartment to start unloading our boxes. My mom had been unable to come with us because she had to attend a writer's conference in Chicago. Miranda and I both agreed that having her parents come with us was a bad idea. Her parents could be a tad bit embarrassing. Since we were doing this together, we decided to be independent and do it without help from anyone else. We had each other.

Now, looking at the stack of boxes and luggage piled in the back of Miranda's Land Rover, I wondered if that had been a mistake. It was going to take us hours to carry all of this stuff up to our dorm room.

"This is gonna take forever," Miranda moaned in frustration.

I started to respond when the loud vibrating sound of really good speakers caught my attention. The source of the music was a small black convertible that had just pulled into the parking space beside us. The first thing I noticed about the driver of the car was her wild blond hair with bright pink tips.

The driver cut the engine, which made my ears instantly thankful. She swung open the door and hopped out of the car. It was obvious from her makeup and attire that she was an emo. She had on heavy black eyeliner and black combat boots. The only thing that threw me off a little was the hair. Hot pink wasn't really an emo thing, was it?

She put one hand on her hip and blew a large bubble with her gum, blatantly staring at both of us. She popped her bubble loudly and smirked. "This shit is gonna be fun," she said in an amused tone, then turned and headed toward the dorm.

Once she was out of hearing range, Miranda grabbed my arm firmly, "Please, God, don't let her live anywhere near us. She scares me."

I couldn't disagree with her there. Nodding, I reached for the closest box to me. "I doubt we'll see her that much. It's a big building. Chances are we aren't even on the same floor. Now, get a box and start unloading."

"I so hope you're right. Should I move to another parking space? You know, away from her," Miranda asked.

"Just grab a box and stop worrying," I replied and resolutely headed for the dorm.

The wild looking blonde was standing on the bottom step watching me when I reached the double doors of the entrance. Great. She hadn't gone inside. I shifted my eyes away from her and to the ground to keep me from tripping and falling.

A loud rumble caused the ground to vibrate. I stumbled and dropped the box of shoes I was carrying. Despite my efforts to hold onto them, the shoes spilled out onto the pavement. I practically growled in frustration. I put my hands on my hips and silently cursed myself for not asking

Miranda's parents to come with us. This was just my first danged box and I couldn't even get it inside safely.

The rumbling sound of a motor became louder and I turned my head to see a black and silver motorcycle come to a halt a few feet away from me and my shoe disaster. It was his fault I'd dropped the danged things. What was he doing riding around campus on a loud motorcycle? When I looked up from the offending motorcycle, my eyes met a pair of brilliant blue eyes. My swift intake of breath was loud, as his gaze traveled over me slowly. He was just so…so…strikingly perfect. Dark thick eyelashes outlined the most insanely blue eyes I'd ever seen. Long dark hair curled at his collar and was tucked behind his ears. A perfect mouth was turned up in a smirk. Wait…a smirk. I shook my head to stop the complete physical assessment I was doing of this stranger. I managed to turn my slightly awed expression to one of annoyance.

"You think you could get a louder motorcycle because I don't think that one woke up the people in Australia?" I snapped and bent down to start picking up my shoes, which was in itself embarrassing.

"Is this my fault?" he asked in a hypnotic sexy drawl. Figures. Guys that looked like that had voices to match.

"You startled me as well as woke up sleeping babies in the surrounding states," I replied throwing one of my cowboy boots into the box.

From the corner of my eye, I saw him stand up and swing one jeans-clad leg over his motorcycle and stand. Great. Now he was coming over here. Just what I needed. I kept my focus on the shoes scattered everywhere as he walked toward me. His black boots stopped just outside my mound of shoes. He bent down and picked up a pink heel that I hardly ever wore. I wasn't even sure why I had brought them. I'd bought them for something, but I couldn't remember what. He picked up the other one and I realized he was holding them almost reverently in his hands. I was curious and couldn't help it. I turned my head to look at him. He was staring down at my pink shoes like something about them made him sad. Did his ex-girlfriend have a pair like that? Or was he just a smoking hot nutso?

"You wanna give me my shoes?" I asked holding out my hand for them. He lifted his gaze and the startling blue color was even more amazing up close. There was sadness there too. I could see it clearly and something in me ached. I didn't even know this guy. Why did I care so deeply about the obvious hurt he was dealing with?

"I like these. I bet they look beautiful on you," he said as he placed both of them carefully in the box.

I wanted to shiver at the husky tone of his voice.

"Thanks," I replied awkwardly. I didn't know what else to say.

"You ready to roll, Dank?" the blonde with pink tipped hair asked as she stepped over my shoes and made her way to his motorcycle. Was she with him? Was he here to get her? The emo girl? Really?

"No, Gee, I'm not," he told her. His attention was flattering and a little nerve-wracking at the same time. It was like he was waiting on me to say or do something. I didn't know what he wanted, but it was hard not to want to do whatever it would take to please him. He reached for another pair of my shoes and put them in the box. He continued until each shoe was back in the correct box. Then he reached down and picked up the box. The snug-fitting black tee shirt he was wearing did wonderful things for his arms as he held the box and stood there waiting for directions.

"Where to?" he asked.

I wasn't sure I wanted *his* help, but I definitely needed help. Miranda was just now making her way across the street. I knew the minute her eyes landed on him. Her mouth dropped open and she dropped the box she was carrying. What the heck? He was hot, but did she have to drop her box and spill her hair products across the street? Dangit. We were never gonna get moved into our dorm room at this rate.

"*Ohmygod,*" she screamed, covering her mouth and doing a little bouncy thing on the balls of her feet. It had moved from embarrassing to humiliating. I was afraid to look back at the guy. Miranda was acting like a lunatic.

"*Miranda*," I hissed, trying to get her to stop going fan-girl over some strange random guy. She then lifted her finger and started pointing at him. Fantastic. She'd gone insane.

"Do you know who he is?" she asked me, and then squealed, still gawking at him.

Did I know who he was? What did she mean? Was I missing something? I turned and looked at him again. He was still just as ridiculously sexy, but he was just a guy. The amused smirk on his face alerted me that maybe he knew why she was acting like she'd lost her mind.

"Who are you?" I asked studying him closely.

The blue in his eyes began to…glow?

"Dank Walker," he replied, never taking his gaze from mine. It was hard to look away from his eyes. Something in them was magnetic. Almost like my body was drawn to him. I didn't like it. It scared me. It was wrong. It wasn't normal.

"Pagan, do you not know who he is? OMG! You have got to be kidding me. I've got to get you out more. I can't believe you are really standing here. Holding Pagan's box. Do you go here? I didn't know you went to college? I am such a big fan. *Yet You Stay* is my ringtone. Love it!"

Ringtone? Wait…

"You're the lead singer in that band," I paused, because I couldn't remember their name. I knew Miranda loved them. I just tuned her out most of the time when she started going on and on about something.

"Cold Soul, Pagan! He is the lead singer of Cold-*freaking*-Soul. How could you not know this?" Miranda informed me as she stepped over her brushes and hair dryer to get closer to Dank Walker.

"I am your biggest fan," she informed him, but I had a feeling he'd figured that much out already.

"It's nice to meet you," he replied politely, but only glanced at her before he turned his attention back to me. The amused grin on his face made me feel like he knew something I didn't. That annoyed me.

"I can take the box. Thanks for your offer to help, but I've got it," I said reaching out to take the box he was holding. He arched one eyebrow and shifted the box out of my reach.

"I'm sure you can handle it all by yourself, Pagan., but I want to carry it to your room. Please." I couldn't be rude. He had said please.

"She wants to carry it herself, Dank. Give her the damn box and let's go. We got stuff to do." The emo girl who was now sitting on his motorcycle called out.

Something that I was pretty sure was anger flashed in his eyes. He didn't even glance back in her direction. "Ignore her," he told me as he nodded his head toward the doors of the dorm. "Lead the way."

I didn't want the wild, slightly scary girl who lived in my dorm to hate me, but Miranda was nudging my arm like an idiot. She wanted me to let Dank Walker carry my box of shoes and he was obviously determined to help me.

"Okay fine, I'll just go get another box. Miranda, you show him where the room is." Miranda beamed at me and nodded her appreciation.

The amused look vanished and Dank Walker seemed annoyed. Fine. Good. He shouldn't be hitting on another girl while he has one on the back of his bike. I wasn't stupid. I knew guys in rock bands were players. That was not my thing.

Miranda began bubbling over with words and more words as she started walking toward the dorm trying very hard to hold Dank's attention. She could handle him. I had no doubt. Heading back to the Land Rover, I tried to block out their voices and focus on the boxes I needed to unload.

CHAPTER TWO

Dank

Three days ago, I'd held her in my arms as she fell asleep telling me about all the things she'd packed. I had teased her about packing too much and not being able to fit it all in her dorm room. She had promised me she would wear those pink high heels on our first official college date. Everything had been perfect. Pagan had loved me.

Now, she didn't even know me.

"Here it is," Miranda announced as she opened the dorm room that I knew connected to Gee's room. I'd made sure of that. I also knew this room was the biggest one available. I wanted Pagan to have the best. I wanted every experience she had to be perfect. She'd been through so much with me already. This was supposed to be the beginning of our happily-ever-after.

"Oh, wow. It's huge! I wonder if this is the right one. We're just freshmen." The excitement in Miranda's voice as she spun around and took in her surroundings reminded me that Miranda had forgotten it all too. My existence in the human world over the past year had been altered. Pagan wouldn't remember. They'd taken that from her. Every memory, gone.

"You can put that box down over there on that side of the room. Pagan will want to be further from the bathroom. It takes me longer to get ready and she can sleep later in the mornings." Miranda was right. Pagan wouldn't spend much time getting ready in the mornings. It also reminded me that I wouldn't be here to hold her and kiss the sleepy look on her face. I placed the box beside her closet. Agony from the separation was slicing through me. Then there was the fear. What if Pagan didn't choose me? What if I never held her again? What if she never looked at me again with love in her eyes? Could I exist without that?

No. I couldn't.

"We're gonna be late," Gee grumbled from the doorway. It was past time we headed out to collect souls. It was just so hard to leave her now that I had her close again. Being unable to touch her or allow her to see me was torture.

"Oh, do you have practice?" Miranda asked batting her eyelashes my way. I'd forgotten she was a Cold Soul fan. I'd been Pagan's boyfriend to her for a while now. The fact she was a fan had faded away. This was going to be annoying.

"No he has a *gig*." Gee explained in an amused drawl.

"Wow, where? Is it sold out? I'd love to go. I've never seen you perform live."

Yeah, she had. Several times., but that was also forgotten. Before I could come up with a suitable reply, Gee interrupted me.

"Pagan is outside talking to a boy. One with a Cajun-talking Daddy, if you know what I mean."

Shit.

I stalked past Miranda and shoved Gee aside as I made my way down to the parking lot in the closest thing to human speed as I could manage, but because I knew Leif was near Pagan and she didn't know who he was or what he had done, I felt this justified a slightly more efficient mode of travel.

I didn't want to scare Pagan by appearing out of thin air. So I came up behind her. Leif felt my presence because his entire body tensed.

"Can I help you carry your things inside?' Leif asked Pagan, looking over her shoulder in an attempt to find me.

I started to take a step forward when Gee grabbed my arm and pulled me back with a hard tug. "Stop it. Remember, he isn't her type. Calm down. Let her handle this. You're going to fuck everything up if you act like some crazed guy with an infatuation. This is not the guy she fell in love with. She fell in love with dark mysterious Dank Walker. She fell in love with Death. Be that guy. Stop being this broken, pitiful, obsessed stalker dude. That won't get her back. And believe it or not, I want Pagan back too."

She was right. I clenched my fists tightly and waited.

"No, thanks. I've got this. It was nice to meet you." Pagan informed him in a slightly annoyed tone that eased my anxiety. Gee was right. Leif wasn't Pagan's type. He never had been. I knew the boy wasn't stupid enough to try to take her again. His father wouldn't allow it. He was testing the waters to see if she really had forgotten.

"See? She's got this. Now, let's go. You act mysterious and sexy. Go get your ass on that motorcycle and drive away without a word."

Leaving Pagan was hard. I didn't want her to have to carry all those things inside. I wanted to do that for her. I was supposed to be the one doing that. She had planned to pay me in sexual favors. We'd joked about it for weeks., but now…she was here. Alone.

"You stay here. Stay near her. Help her move in. Most importantly, keep the Voodoo prince away from her. I'll be back as soon as non-humanly possible."

Surprisingly, Gee didn't argue.

Pagan

"Smart move. He looked like a creep."

The blonde with the pink tipped hair was suddenly beside me. I hadn't heard her walk up, but I'd been busy trying to get rid of the overly friendly guy who had met me at Miranda's car and wouldn't take a hint.

"He was nice enough. I'm just not crazy about giving directions to my room to every guy on campus," I explained. And I didn't want them to feel as if I owed them something for their help.

The girl reached into the car and pulled out my suitcase. I wasn't sure what to think about that. The roar of the motorcycle's engine startled me and I spun around too see Dank Walker drive away without so much as a glance my way. Not that I expected it, really. I mean, he had been very nice and seemed somewhat interested, but I didn't exactly encourage him.

"Weren't you going with him?" I asked as the girl walked around me with a suitcase handle in one hand and one of my boxes tucked in her other arm. She was really going to help me unload? Why? I'd done nothing to win her favor. She didn't appear to be someone who made friends easily.

"Changed my mind. He's in a bit of a funk today," she said without looking back at me. I watched as she made her way to the entrance of the dorm then I turned around and grabbed a box myself. She wouldn't know which room to go to and even if she found the room on her own, it would terrify Miranda if emo girl walked into the room when she was there alone.

* * * *

Two hours later we were completely unpacked. Even our very large room was set up. We'd taken the empty boxes to the dumpster, packed the fridge with water bottles, and I'd given half my closet space to Miranda. She'd brought too many clothes to fit in hers. This was not surprising in the least. I figured that it would be easier to live with a jam-packed closet than listening to Miranda whine for the next nine months because her closet wasn't big enough. Besides, with the size of this room, we could easily fit one of those portable closets in the corner.

"I still can't believe she is in the room connected to ours and she doesn't have to share with anyone. What is she? A rock star's kid? *That's it!* She is some famous rocker's kid. She looks the part. She is obviously on a first name basis with Dank Walker and she has the money and power to have her very own dorm room. And she has that weird name. Who calls their kid 'Gee' but some famous person?"

Most times, I waved Miranda's ridiculous ideas away, but this time she just might be right. No one else in the dorm had her own room, everyone else had a roommate. Granted, our room was huge. It was even bigger than Gee's, but we were sharing it. I plopped down on my black polka-dotted comforter that Miranda had insisted I get. She wanted us to match. Hers was black with white polka dots and mine was white with black polka dots. I didn't really care for the pattern, but honestly, I'd have been fine with a quilt from home as my cover. Miranda had thrown a hissy fit when I'd suggested that. So, we now had polka dots. Everything else was black and white too. Black and white was her current decorating color scheme obsession. She had even bought us matching pin boards with black and white ribbon on them to hang above our desks, right beside the black and white dry erase boards.

"It looks good, doesn't it?" She asked smugly as she sat down beside me. She was happy with the way everything had fit into place. I was just glad she'd left the *One Direction* posters at her house. I don't like boy bands and I sure don't want to them plastered over the walls of my room all year.

"You did a good job," I agreed and she beamed at me. It didn't take much to make her smile. She'd gone through a rough patch there for a while after her boyfriend, Wyatt, had passed away. It had been the three of us growing up. Losing him had hurt me, too, but not as badly as it had her. They had a connection I didn't share. Shopping for our room had kept her busy over the past month and she'd slowly started to heal.

"What should we do now? Want to go check out the campus? Or go find something to eat? The campus food court doesn't open until tomorrow. We'll have to leave campus to find dinner."

I started to answer when Gee walked into the room through the bathroom that adjoined our rooms. "I know the perfect place to go eat and have a little fun. Let's go, bitches."

Chapter Three

Pagan

Although it was an age-restricted club, Gee had gotten us inside without a hitch. I'd started to refuse to go in, but Miranda had gotten all excited when the bouncer waved us through. I had to follow them in to keep Miranda out of trouble.

"Stop frowning, Peggy Ann. It ain't that bad. Loosen up," Gee said as we made our way toward one of the empty tables.

"My name is Pagan," I informed her.

"You used to be more fun," she mumbled. What the heck did she mean by that? We'd known each other all of six hours tops. I was about to ask about her comment when a guy stepped in front of me.

"Hey, beautiful. You're new here. I'd remember eyes like those if I'd seen them before."

I let out a weary sigh and looked up at him. "Really? That's the best you've got?" I asked raising an eyebrow.

His confused frown annoyed me and I stepped around him.

"Harsh! I like it." Gee chuckled as we took our seats at the bar.

Miranda grabbed my arm and jerked me close to her, "Don't look now, but Jay is here," she whispered excitedly in my ear.

I knew Jay went to University of Tennessee, which was just one city over from us, but I hadn't expected to bump into him so soon, especially not on my first night in college. I started to look back, but Miranda squeezed my arms tightly. "I said don't look. He's with a girl. They're dancing really close and, well, I think she may be humping his leg."

"What do you want to drink, Pay-gan," Gee asked in a mocking voice, drawing my name out since I'd corrected her before.

"A Coke will be fine," I said and turned my attention away from Miranda's death grip on my arm to Gee, who was perched on a barstool as if she were actually old enough to order something more than a soda.

"You want Coke? Why am I not surprised?" she replied with a roll of her eyes. Her gaze shifted from me to something over my shoulder. "Well, shit," she mumbled.

Curious, I turned around and my eyes met Jay's. He was in fact dancing with some blond girl who just might have been humping his leg. His hands were cupping her butt and he was whispering something in her ear, or at least he had been until he saw me. His surprised expression made me smile. I'm sure he had no idea I was at Boone. I hadn't spoken to him since Wyatt's funeral. I smiled and gave him a little wave and turned around to look at Gee. She was watching me closely as if she may need to tackle me to the ground at any given moment. What was her deal? She was just weird enough to make me nervous.

"You know him?" she asked, shifting her eyes from me to Jay's direction.

Shrugging, I picked up the Coke the bartender placed in front of me. "Yeah, he used to go to my school," I explained. I didn't want to explain to her that he had also been my boyfriend for three years. She would probably embarrass me somehow with that information.

"He was her boyfriend for three years. They were inseparable," Miranda chimed in with her juicy piece of gossip. I'd have to thank her later for that one.

"Hmmm…well, Pay-gan, you need to decide what you want to do because here he comes," Gee replied. She seemed annoyed.

Great.

"Pagan?" Jay's surprised tone had me wishing I'd stayed in my dorm room tonight. I was not up for this right now. Especially with Gee watching my every move.

I took a deep breath, forced a smile on my face, and turned around to face Jay.

"Hello, Jay."

"Hiya, Jay. Fancy meeting you here," Miranda said with a giggle.

" I can't believe y'all are here," Jay said with a huge grin on his face. "What are you doing here?"

"We're both at Boone," I explained.

"Boone? Really? As in you're living only thirty minutes from me?" The excitement in his voice surprised me. We'd been broken up over a year and a half now. It wasn't like we were long lost friends.

"Yep. Moved in today," Miranda said before taking a sip of her Shirley Temple. At least, I hoped it was a Shirley Temple. Surely Gee hadn't ordered her something with alcohol in it.

"Were you gonna call me? Clue me in that you are right around the corner?" Jay's focus was on me, but I was watching the blonde who had been humping his leg. From the look on her face, she wasn't very happy. I watched her approach us and wrap her arms around Jay's arm. I shifted my eyes from her angry glare to his suddenly tense one.

"So, who are your friends, Jay Jay?" the blonde asked, pressing closer against him.

I had to bite my lip to keep from laughing at "Jay Jay". Miranda kicked me and I heard her muffled chuckle. She was getting a kick out of the nickname too.

"Uh, this is, uh—" he stammered.

I decided to save him from his moment of panic and smiled over at his new girlfriend. "Hello. I'm Pagan and this is Miranda. We went to high school with Jay." I'd wanted to say "Jay Jay" so badly, but I refrained because I knew if I did, I would burst into laughter.

She reached up and ran her hand through Jay's shaggy blond hair while keeping her eyes locked on me. Apparently, I was the one she was least fond of. "Is that so? He never mentioned either of you."

That was a little surprising. Since we'd broken up the summer he left to come up here for college. I figured he would have at least missed me a little. Guess I thought wrong. I shrugged. "Must not have ranked real high on his importance radar," I replied.

I shifted my eyes to Jay's and smirked. I was done with this fun conversation. I could see the frown puckering his forehead and decided to get away while I could. The last thing I wanted was for him or Miranda to delve into our past.

"It was nice seeing you again, maybe we'll bump into each other again over the next three years." I turned back around in my stool and let my fake smile dissolve. Now, it was his turn to walk away. We'd had our little weird moment. Time to move on.

"Is your cell number still the same?" Jay asked. Dang it. Did the boy not take a hint? I was not interested in him. He had moved on. Jeez.

"Yep. Her number hasn't changed," Miranda replied when it was obvious I wasn't going to.

This time I kicked Miranda.

"Ouch!" she squealed.

"Get rid of them," I whispered to Gee who was sitting there surprisingly quiet watching the whole thing.

She winked at me and turned her attention back to Jay. "Looks like Pagan isn't up for any more chit-chat, Jay Jay. So you and your girlfriend can get back to humping on the dance floor. It was entertaining us earlier."

I covered my face with my hands. Why had I trusted her to handle this?

Miranda burst into a fit of giggles and spun around on her stool away from them too. I kept my eyes closed tightly hoping they'd just walk away. I did not want Jay to think I'd been watching him dirty dance.

"They are gone. You're welcome," Gee announced and raised her empty glass in the air rattling the ice around. "He's kinda cute, but I'm thinking that chick he has hanging on him has silver-tipped nails ready to slice open anyone who gets close."

"I picked up on that," I replied and drank the last of the soda in my glass.

"He is so still into you," Miranda said nudging my arm. Was she blind? Jay was very taken. He had always been polite and friendly to everyone. Of course he would be like that toward us. We'd all done everything together from the time we'd been freshman to the year he graduated before us.

"No, he isn't. Besides, I'm not looking."

Miranda sighed and made a pouty face. "You're never looking. You weren't even aware of the sexiness that is Dank Walker today."

That was where she was wrong. I was very aware of how sexy Dank Walker had been. It would take a blind person to miss that and even then, they would probably be able to tell. His voice was hypnotic. But he was a lead singer in a rock band. Not my type. His kind wanted a girl only long enough to get her naked and in bed. Then he moved on.

"I noticed. I just didn't care. I don't do rockers. That's your thing."

Gee cleared her throat and I turned my attention to her. "What you got against musicians?"

"The fact that they want a different girl every night. Sex, drugs, and rock 'n' roll," I replied.

Gee studied me a moment, then nodded her head slowly as if she agreed. "Maybe, but Dank isn't your typical lead singer."

"Sure he isn't," I replied, letting the sarcasm drip from my tone. "I'm not in the mood to talk about this. How long do we have to stay here?"

"We just got here, Pagan. A cute guy hasn't even asked me to dance yet," Miranda whined, glancing over both her shoulders for any males who may be checking her out so she could pounce.

"Okay, fine. We'll wait until you get to dance, then can we leave?"

"You got boring, Peggy Ann," Gee mumbled.

What was it with her calling me Peggy Ann? She knew my name was Pagan. And why did she keep referring to me as if we had known each other for longer than half a day? Did she do drugs? She had been on the back of Dank Walker's motorcycle once today. Maybe she was a groupie. Didn't groupies do drugs and sleep with the band?

"Oh, boys!" Miranda squealed quietly and tugged on my arm. Two boys were standing behind us. One of them looked familiar; I must have seen him somewhere before.

"It's nice to meet you, Nathan," Miranda said in her sweet voice. The one she thought was sexy and only used when an attractive guy was talking to her. The familiar one was very focused on her. He ran a hand through his dark brown hair that curled on the ends giving it a messy look. I liked him. I wasn't sure why exactly, but I approved.

"This is my friend Pagan," Miranda announced to the boys. "Pagan, these are Nathan and Kent. They both go to UT."

Kent took a step toward me. "If you dance with me, I think your friend will dance with Nathan, and if you've noticed, he's practically drooling. He hasn't taken his eyes off her since y'all walked in here." The teasing grin on his face as he looked at Nathan alleviated any worry I had. He wasn't hitting on me. He was here as Nathan's wingman. I stood up and took the hand that Kent had held out to me.

"I'd love to dance," I smiled back at Miranda, "throw the boy a bone." I told her causing her to laugh as she stood up and slipped her hand in Nathan's. He was staring at her as if he'd just been gifted some rare jewel. I liked that. A lot. So far, Nathan had my approval.

"By all means, you two run along and dance. I'll just sit here and drink," Gee said reminding me she was there. Feeling guilty, I looked back at her, but she had an amused smirk on her face, so I knew she was teasing. Besides, Gee was a rock band groupie. She didn't do college boys.

"We'll be back soon," I assured her.

She held up her newest drink, "I'm fine and dandy right here. Please go entertain yourselves. Maybe you'll lighten up, Peggy Ann."

I rolled my eyes at her continued use of her nickname for me. I realized that I would always be Peggy Ann to her. She wasn't going to stop calling me that.

"Let's dance," I said turning to Kent.

He led me onto the crowded dance floor. Bodies were moving everywhere. Most of them were just as intense as Jay and his girlfriend had been. I really hoped Kent wasn't expecting me to rub all over him. That wasn't the kind of dancing I'd signed up for.

"I saw you talking to Potts earlier. You know him?"

He knew Jay. UT was a big place. How odd. "Uh, yeah. Jay and I went to high school together."

Kent pulled us into the thick of things and slipped a hand around my waist. I wasn't sure I liked that. "Really? That's cool. Jay and I are ATO brothers."

Ah. A frat boy. Great.

"Are you at UT?" he asked with interest.

"Nope. I'm at Boone."

Kent slid his hand down my hip and pulled me against him as the music slowed to a sexy beat. I did not like this. I searched the crowd until I found Miranda to see how she and Nathan were doing. She was wrapped in Nathan's arms and looking at him like he was the most handsome guy she'd ever seen. I wanted her to have this time. She needed to have some fun and begin to go out with other boys. But could I deal with Kent rubbing all over me to give her that time?

Just then two larger hands slid around my waist and held me firmly. Warm breath tickled my neck and instead of being startled by it, it excited me. "Time's up," a deep sexy drawl said from behind me. Kent's eyes went wide.

"Are you…are you…*holy shit!* You're Dank Walker. Cold Soul's Dank Walker." Kent's arms immediately let go of me as he stepped back. His eyes were focused on the guy behind me. Why Dank Walker was standing behind me making some big claim on me I wasn't sure, but at the moment I was just glad that Kent was no longer pressing his pelvis against me.

"Yeah. Now go," Dank replied. Kent nodded his head and backed away into the moving bodies.

Turning around. I frowned at him. The relieved look on his face surprised me. "What was that about?" I asked.

Dank's eyes changed from a simmering whirlpool as he watched Kent walk away to a soft glow as he looked at me. "He was making you uncomfortable."

How had he known that? "Maybe. But why do you care?"

Dank let out a frustrated sigh and shook his head, "I don't know. But I do."

Okay…That was unexpected.

"Will you dance with me, Pagan?"

I studied Dank as he watched me carefully, waiting on my answer. I didn't trust guys like him. No female should. But I couldn't turn him down. I slipped a hand over his arm. His hands were still on my waist.

The music instantly slowed. The sexual beat of the music had changed to something easy and smooth. I eased into his arms and trust came easily. Dank's hands didn't wander. He didn't make vulgar moves with his body. Instead, he held me closely as we moved to the music.

The smell of his shirt was something dark and exotic. I wanted to bury my nose in it and breathe in the scent. This guy could be dangerous. Every part of him was irresistible. Turning my head slightly so I could smell him better, I was startled when a soft growl vibrated against his chest. What was that?

I looked at him and saw his eyes were now cold and hard, and they were focused on something behind me. I glanced over my shoulder and saw Jay standing there. His hands were jammed in his pockets and his girlfriend was missing from his arm. He was looking at me. I turned from Dank's arms and faced Jay. Did he need something?

"Hey, Jay," I said trying to ease the sudden tension. Did they know each other?

"Pagan. I wanted to see if you would dance with me for old times' sake. I didn't realize you were uh, with Dank Walker. Wow, you moved up in the world."

I laughed. These boys were really into Dank's band. "I'm not with Dank. We just met today. I'd love to dance with you as long as your girlfriend doesn't mind. Let me finish this dance first though."

Jay shifted his eyes from me to Dank, then back to me again quickly. "Yeah, sure. I'll be waiting."

I gave him a reassuring smile because he suddenly seemed really nervous. Odd, Jay wasn't the nervous type. I turned around and put my hands back on Dank's arms. The muscles flexed under my touch and my imagination took off. He would be incredible without a shirt on. I didn't have to see it to know it.

"You know him," Dank said in a slow even tone.

"Yes. We went to high school together," I explained, purposely leaving out that he'd been my one and only boyfriend. Dank seemed annoyed with Jay. I was probably imagining it, but I was going to protect Jay just in case. For a musician, Dank Walker was really built.

"Do you like him?" Dank asked.

Well, that was very blunt. I stopped dancing and stared up at him. "I don't think that is really your business. We just met today."

Dank bit his bottom lip and, dad-gum, if that wasn't hot as hell. I really wanted to pull that bottom lip out and suck on it. I was just as bad as any other groupie. I'd just met the guy and I was thinking bad thoughts.

"Okay. You're right. I'm sorry," he replied.

The sad expression in his eyes made my heart hurt. I squelched the desire to reach up and touch his face. I didn't want him to be sad. Had I sounded mean? I hadn't meant to.

"Let's just dance," I said as the music began another sexy beat.

Dank nodded and his hands slid down further over my hips as he pulled me closer. The smooth easy way his body moved with mine made my heart speed up with excitement. His hands left my waist and circled my wrist. I looked up at him as he took my hands and pulled them up to wrap around his neck, pressing my body closer to his. The dark sultry gleam in his eyes made my breath hitch. I wasn't experienced enough to play in his world. But no matter how dangerous he could be for my heart, I couldn't seem to break free from the hypnotic spell he had me under.

"Alright, lover boy, why don't you lay off the heavy with Peggy Ann here? You have places to go and people to see." Gee's voice brought me back to reality. I let my hands fall from behind his neck and I took a step back.

"Gee," the warning in his tone caused me to shiver.

"Don't go getting all pissy. I'm just reminding you of your plans," she replied putting emphasis on the last word. What exactly was Gee to Dank Walker?

Chapter Four

Dank

I am going to strangle Gee. Pagan was warming up to me. She was in my arms and I had found a modicum of peace from the fear that had gripped me since the moment I found out I could lose her.

"Dank," Gee replied saucily. I knew she was right. I hadn't finished taking souls for the night, but I'd known Pagan was here. I could feel her emotions. Her soul still called out to me even though she no longer remembered me.

"Um, I'll leave you two to work this out. I promised Jay a dance anyway," Pagan said backing away.

Don't leave me.

Pagan froze. Damn. I'd spoken to her soul. She'd heard me. The confusion in her eyes as she studied me made me hope she remembered; that her human brain was overpowered by her soul. But she shook her head and continued moving away. "I gotta go," she said hastily, then spun around and fled.

"Smart move, asshole. You just scared the shit outta her," Gee said with a sigh.

"Why'd you interrupt us? I know my duty. I don't need you to screw with this."

Gee raised both her blond pierced eyebrows. "Oh, really? Well, if you would only stop lusting over Pagan long enough to remember that you have a job to do. You have to let her make her own choices. If you did that, I wouldn't have to step in. Yeah, you had her all wrapped up in that sexy, dark spell thing you have going on. But her soul is connected to Jay's. She needs to face that. Then she has to decide. You can't come in and intercept her every time she gets close to him."

Snarling, I stalked toward the exit. I didn't need to hear this. She was right and I hated that she was right. Pagan had to get close to Jay again. This was a competition. One I may very well lose. I winced as the pain sliced through me. Losing Pagan wasn't something I could accept.

I glanced at the dance floor and my eyes immediately found Pagan's. She was watching me go. Jay wasn't with her. She stood alone on the outside of the moving bodies, her attention completely focused on me. I stopped and stared back at her. I took in the tilt of her head, the softness of her lips and the interest in her eyes. I'd intrigued her tonight. That was a good thing. Would the Pagan who didn't see souls on a daily basis be as accepting of Death as the one who had grown up seeing a part of this world that others were blind to? Jay came up behind her and touched her shoulder and she turned back to look at him. I couldn't stay to watch this.

Pagan

"Am I gonna get that dance now?" Jay asked loudly over the music.

I glanced back at Dank to see if he was still there. He seemed sad or lonely. I wanted to go talk to him. But he was gone. It was not a good idea to be interested in a lead singer. Yes, he was hard to ignore, but it was in my best interest to find a way to get over his appeal.

"Yes, I—" I stopped mid-sentence. The girlfriend was back and she was slipping her hands around Jay's waist. Jay's frustration was obvious on his face.

"Come dance with me," she cooed as she slid both her hands underneath his shirt. Yep, that was enough for me.

"I need to go. It was nice to see you again," I said quickly and made my escape before he could say any more. Scanning the bar, I found Gee sitting there with her legs crossed and a smirk on her face. Miranda was still dancing with Nathan. As much as I wanted to leave, I didn't want to end the night early for Miranda. She was obviously having a good time. I made my way over to Gee. Maybe I could just get a taxi home and leave her here with Miranda.

"What happened with frat boy number two?" Gee asked as she took another sip of her drink.

"I'm ready to go. If I get a taxi, can you wait around on Miranda?"

Gee shrugged, "Yeah, I guess. It's still pretty early. Why are you heading out already?"

Because the guy I wanted to be dancing with was gone.

"I'm tired. It's been a long day," I replied.

"Okay. See ya later then," Gee replied and wiggled her long black nails at me.

I looked back to check on Miranda one last time; the smile on her face as she talked to the Nathan guy was my answer. She was fine. Good for her.

* * * *

Smoke was everywhere. I was lost inside of it. I couldn't panic. If I wanted to survive this, I couldn't panic. My chest felt tight from the lack of oxygen. Slowly, I waded through the smoke, praying I'd make it out before the darkness took over. A small light appeared through the thickness and hope pushed me harder. My legs felt heavy. The closer I got to the light the slower my body moved. It was becoming harder to pick up my legs and put one in front of the other. My knees buckled and I realized I wasn't going to make it. The light was there. So close. But I wasn't going to get to it. The smoke was going to claim me. I took another strangled breath as my knees hit the cement underneath me.

Strong arms encircled me and the suffocation was lifted. I took a deep clear breath. The arms held me close to a firm warm chest. I tried to open my eyes, but I couldn't.

"You're okay. I'm here." The deep voice assured me. *I knew that voice. I gripped the shirt that covered the body that held me. I wanted to see him. I knew him.*

"Help," I begged. *My eyes wouldn't open.*

"Always. You're fine. This is just a bad dream. I'm here." He assured me. *I believed him. I couldn't see him, but my body knew it was safe. Relaxing in his arms, I breathed deeply again.*

"I want to see you," I told him.

"I wish you could. You will again one day." His confusing reply was the last thing he said before the loud blaring alarm went off.

My eyes snapped open and I was staring at the ceiling of my dorm room.

"Turn that off," Miranda grumbled, throwing a pillow at the alarm clock beside my bed. We had freshman orientation in an hour. I reached over and pressed snooze. Bits of a dream flitted through my memory. I wanted to remember it. Something about it had excited me. But I couldn't remember what exactly. Sitting on the edge of my bed, I thought hard about the moment before my alarm clock had gone off. There was something I wanted to remember, but I couldn't recall it. I was drawing a blank.

Frustrated, I threw the covers off and stood up. Miranda had huddled down deeper in her covers. I had no idea what time she'd finally gotten home last night. She was almost impossible to wake up when she'd had sufficient sleep. This morning was going to be difficult. I decided I'd get a shower first, then I'd try to get her to wake up. Attending orientation was required. She'd have to get up and get there even if she only had enough time to brush her teeth and put on wrinkled clothes.

Gee was standing in front of the mirror. She wasn't looking in it. Her back was turned to it and she was leaning against the counter with her arms crossed in front of her like she'd was waiting on someone. Her hair was already styled—well, as much as she styled it—and she was dressed. She'd been out later than me. How did she look so awake?

"Sleeping in, Peggy Ann?" She asked not moving from her spot in front of the sink. I really needed to have a shower, but I wasn't one to strip down in front of other people.

"Yeah, I can't believe you're so awake. But since you are up and dressed, could you get out so I could do the same?"

Gee pushed off from her stance against the counter. "Snippy, snippy. I guess you don't want to hear about the private invite you got to attend Cold Soul's concert Friday night either."

I watched as Gee started walking toward the door to give me privacy like I'd asked. I shouldn't ask her about the concert. I didn't date musicians. It was a bad idea.

"Wait. What do you mean? Did Dank invite me?" I was weak. The guy was hard to resist.

Gee halted in her steps and grinned. "Yeah. He did. You even get to bring your friend along if you want to. Backstage passes and all."

Backstage. That meant he wanted to see me. Didn't it? I didn't need to entertain these thoughts, but he made it so hard to remember that he was a bad boy. He didn't act like one. He seemed almost lonely or lost. Not like the wild playboy I'd decided he was from day one.

"Okay. I want to go. I'm sure Miranda will want to go too." I wanted to ask her why he hadn't called me himself or if I could have his number, but he hadn't offered that and maybe I shouldn't ask.

"I'll let him know. But then again, you may see him first," Gee replied then opened the door and closed it behind her before I could ask her what she meant.

Dank

I had been waiting for her since I'd left her bedroom this morning. Last night had been the first time I'd gone into Pagan's dreams. It felt like an invasion of privacy that I'd never wanted to cross. But while I sat there watching her sleep and making sure she was safe, she'd started to have a bad dream. It had taken me a few moments to decide whether or not I should go into her dream and ease her fears or physically hold her like I used to when she was having a nightmare. I decided that the safer way to be with her was in her dreams.

The moment her alarm had gone off, I left. She'd be arriving at this building soon. I stepped around the tree I'd been leaning against and made myself visible. College girls liked lead singers. I had to dodge overly aggressive females when I was on campus.

"Dank Walker? No way. I'd heard you'd been seen on campus, but I didn't believe it. But here you are," a female had already noticed me. She began scrambling through her book bag. "I have a Sharpie in here somewhere. Could you autograph my bag or my shirt, oh better yet—my bra?" she said as she pulled a Sharpie from her book bag.

The girl had started lifting her shirt up before it dawned on me that she was serious about the bra.

"No. I don't sign bras," I held the pen she'd handed me and moved my attention from her to the students approaching the building. My eyes locked with Pagan's. Shit. She saw that the girl's damn shirt had been up. I shoved the Sharpie back in her direction without breaking eye contact with Pagan and stepped around her. "I gotta go," was the only explanation I gave her.

Pagan turned her head and stared straight ahead and hurried toward the building. I wasn't going to let her get inside without talking to me.

Talk to me Pagan. Please.

She halted. Talking in her head was unfair, but I hated not being able to show her who I was. I wanted her to see me. I wanted her to love me anyway.

"Good morning, Pagan," I said as I stopped beside her. She tilted her head to the side and peered up at me. The startled, confused look in her eyes made me feel guilty. I shouldn't have spoken to her that way. She wasn't ready.

"Dank?" Her voice sounded as if she were asking a question.

I reached for her book bag, and in her still confused state she let me take it. Slinging it over my shoulder, I nodded toward the entrance to the building that Pagan's calculus class would be in for the next semester. "Better hurry or you'll be late."

She shook her head, then her eyes zoned in on the book bag now over my shoulder. A small frown puckered her brow. "What are you doing?" she asked.

"Taking your books inside. It looked heavy," I started walking before she could decide she wanted her book bag back. I was carrying it inside. I wanted every male in the vicinity to see me carrying her bag. I already had to deal with the soul mate. I didn't want to be forced to see her with anyone else. I was staking my claim.

"Oh. Well, yeah. We got a lot of info at freshman orientation, then I had to go to the bookstore and pick up some books I didn't have. This is the only class I have today. Apparently, this professor is anal and doesn't want to miss one day of class."

I loved hearing her talk. When we got to the door, I opened it and stepped back so that she could walk in. She glanced back toward the tree where I'd been standing when she walked up and then back at me. "I saw you with a girl and she was taking off her clothes for you? Did she change her mind and decide that stripping in public was a bad idea?"

The cute teasing note to her voice made me smile. "She wanted me to sign her bra. I told her I don't sign bras; then I saw you and handed her back her marker so I could catch up with you before you got away."

"Oh," she replied and stopped at the door marked 312. "And why don't you sign bras?"

Was Pagan flirting with me? Damn, that mischievous twinkle in her eyes drove me a little crazy. I closed the distance between us and bent my head down until my mouth was right beside her ear. "There's only one bra I'd like to sign." Pagan's breathing hitched and I smiled to myself before standing back up. I wanted a taste. It had been too long since I'd had a taste of her mouth...of her skin.

I stepped inside the classroom desperate to get hold of myself. Inhaling her scent had made my senses go on high alert. Pagan stepped inside while I held the door for her. The jeans she wore cupped her ass like a second skin.

It was impossible not to watch as she walked across the room. Jerking my gaze from her, I scanned the other students to see who else was watching her. I didn't want them looking.

CHAPTER FIVE

Pagan

Was he talking in my head, or had I lost my mind? I hadn't been able to focus on anything my calculus professor had said. Luckily, it was a brief welcome and an overview of the syllabus. Then we'd been dismissed. I was sure I'd missed something important, but Dank Walker had been sitting beside me. Every female eye in the room was on him and my body tingled every time he brushed his arm against mine, and it seemed that happened a lot. Almost as if he knew what it did to me and he made sure to do it just enough to keep me frazzled.

My book bag was still slung over his arm so, as we left, I was forced to endure every fan who stopped him to ask about his concert, to slip him their number and promise him everything from a deep throat to a strip show. If it wasn't for the fact I really wanted my book bag and I wanted to see if he talked in my head again now that I was fully awake so I could gauge whether or not that had been real, I'd have walked off and left him to his adoring fans.

"Follow me," Dank said as he took my arm and steered me away from a girl in midsentence. I had to run to keep up with him as he led me toward a large oak tree behind the building. There was a picnic table underneath it. Was he hiding?

"They won't notice me back here," he explained, making sure the tree was blocking him from the view of everyone else before he sat down on the picnic table. Something about seeing him sitting there seemed familiar. Almost as if I were experiencing a déjà vu. He smirked as if he'd read my mind.

"I'm surprised you walked off and left that last girl. If you'd brought her back here, I am more than positive you'd have gotten some pretty naughty action. She was getting ready to offer to carry your first born."

Dank chuckled and shook his head, "I'll pass. Not my type."

So far I wasn't sure what his type was. Not only did he seem to be stalking me, but I hadn't see him with anyone else. Was it because I was a challenge?

"Why the interest in me? If I offer to strip for you, will that send you running away? Am I the type of toy you never got to play with?" I made sure to smile as I asked. I didn't want to sound like a jerk, but I really wanted to know why me. There were plenty of girls available who were more than willing to do what he wanted, when he wanted it. Dank let my bag drop to the wooden planks of the picnic table and slowly stood up. His eyes were focused on me and the intensity of his gaze almost scared me. Sometimes his eyes didn't seem real. They seemed unnatural—beautifully unnatural and haunting.

"Understand this, Pagan Moore," he began in a deep sexy voice, "if you ever offer to strip for me, then you will have my complete, undivided attention."

Oh my.

Swallowing hard, I managed to give a semblance of a nod. Dank didn't back away. Instead, he moved closer until I was pressed against the tree. "You aren't a game. You will never be a game to me," he said as he traced my jawline with the tip of his finger. The longing in his eyes was too strong. It didn't make sense. We'd just met each other yesterday. Why did he react this way to me? And why did my heart go crazy when he got close?

"It's been too long. I can't not kiss you," he whispered before his mouth covered mine. His words made no sense, but that faded to the back of my mind when his tongue slid into my mouth and the rich decadent foreign taste teased my senses. My hands flew up to his shoulders and I held on for dear life. My knees were weak and I needed support, but mainly, I just wanted to keep him there. Just like this. I inhaled the warm dark scent that engulfed me as his body crowded mine. His teeth grazed my bottom lip and I whimpered as his lips began kissing the spot behind my ear. The heat of his breath tickled my skin. Gripping his shirt tightly, I pressed closer. One of his knees slid between my legs and settled between them, causing sparks of pleasure to shoot through me.

"Ah," I cried out as he moved his knee higher. My body trembled in response. Dank buried his head in the curve between my neck and shoulder. His heavy breathing accompanied by his sudden stillness told me this was about to end. I didn't want it to end, but then again, the way I was reacting to an innocent kiss might mean I wasn't ready for Dank Walker's kisses after all. I started to move and his arms tightened their hold on my waist.

"No. Please. Not yet. Let me have this," the pleading sound in his voice as his words were spoken against my skin compelled me to do as he asked. Who could say no to that?

His heavy breathing made very naughty thoughts run through my head. His arms slid around me and pulled me closer as his knee lowered, but his leg stayed there between mine. "Are you coming Friday night? I want you there," he said as he finally lifted his head to look at me.

He wasn't my type. He wasn't safe. But I didn't care. I was a college student. I'd been safe long enough. It was time I gave in a little to the wild side. "Yes, I'll be there."

Dank closed his eyes in relief and a smile tugged the corner of his lips. "I was prepared to bribe you. That was easier than I thought," he replied.

"Bribe me, huh? Maybe I should have held out longer."

Dank's eyes lowered and studied my lips. "What do you want, Pagan? Just ask."

Whoa. He was once again a little too intense.

"Um, well, right now I want to take a nap because I didn't get nearly enough sleep last night." I was sure that was not the answer he'd been hoping for, but it was true.

Dank stepped back and I suddenly felt cold. "Don't let Gee make you do things you don't want to. She doesn't require as much sleep as you do."

Were they related? Nothing else made sense. She seemed close to him, but they weren't a couple or anything remotely close to that. "I'm a big girl. I can handle Gee."

Dank let out a short sexy laugh and nodded, "Yeah. I know."

Dank

"She doesn't remember you either. I expected her to forget me. But why doesn't she remember you?" I'd felt his arrival, but I had waited until Pagan was far enough away to turn around and look at him.

Leif stood several feet away from me. I had thought taking her from him with the threat of ending his world would be enough to keep him away. The boy was verging on stupid. "She isn't your concern. I suggest you go back to Vilokan and play with your friends there. My patience with you is wearing thin, Voodoo *prince*."

He glared at me and crossed his arms over his chest. "I'm not doing anything wrong. I've left her alone. I just came to see if she was okay. Before you showed up, protecting Pagan had been the only life I'd ever known."

Leif had been Pagan's dark angel. One she hadn't known existed. His sick and twisted claim on her soul had been something I'd fought his father, the Voodoo lord of the dead, for in his own dwelling.

"You've screwed with Pagan's future enough. She is just now learning what a normal human life is like. I'm the only one that she needs to assure her protection. I won't tolerate your hanging around. This isn't your business."

Leif started to say more when Gee appeared by my side. "Well, look what Hell dragged in," she said with a sigh and plopped down on the table. "Do I need to make sure you boys play nice? Because I will and I'll enjoy every second of it."

Leif's glare turned to one of hatred when he shifted his focus to Gee. There was no love lost between the two of them. "She doesn't remember you either," Leif snarled.

"Ooooh look, Dankmar! He's still just as quick as he ever was. Doesn't that just make us the lucky ones?"

"I'm not leaving until one of you explain to me what is wrong with Pagan," Leif demanded.

Gee cackled and I knew her small bout of humor was running thin. The Voodoo prince was pushing it. "Pagan is fine. She is finding herself without the claim of evil on her soul."

Leif started to take a step forward and Gee was in his face in less than a tenth of a second. She'd moved at non-human speed and I looked around quickly to make sure no one had seen it.

"You take one more step this way and I *will cut you*," she hissed.

"You need to leave. This is your final warning."

Leif didn't argue. He was gone.

Gee cursed and spun around to look at me, "Dammit. I was hoping he'd stay here. That woulda been fun. I've been wanting to beat his Voodoo ass for a year now."

"That would have been fun to watch, " I agreed. "But we need to get to work. There's been an earthquake in Haiti. It's a bad one."

Gee sighed, "Guess you're taking me too this time."

Surprised at her lack of enthusiasm, I stopped and raised an eyebrow her way.

"Oh, don't look at me like that. Can I help it if I like being a college student? It's a helluva lot more fun than dealing with dead people."

Chapter Six

Pagan

Miranda was standing in front of her closet with several outfits laying over both our beds and desks when I walked into the room. I'd spent the rest of the day checking out my classes, meeting with professors, and finding a coffee shop close enough to stop by in the mornings on my way to each class.

"Did our closets throw up?" I asked as I closed the door behind me and took in the mess in front of me.

"Maybe," she nibbled on her bottom lip nervously. "I have nothing to wear. Nothing."

I knew for a fact she had enough clothes to clothe a small country. What she meant was she didn't have anything to wear on a date. Must be someone she really liked because I hadn't seen her go this crazy over what to wear in years.

"Who's the lucky guy?" I asked, moving over a blue denim skirt that belonged to me and her royal blue scarf shirt so I could sit down on my bed.

"Nathan. The guy from the club," Miranda clapped her hands excitedly, "and get this! He is in the same fraternity as Jay. They want both of us to go out to dinner tonight and go see a movie."

Uh-oh. That wasn't going to work.

"Um, well, see, here is the thing. Jay has a girlfriend or is obviously in a relationship. I saw it last night at the club. You know I don't do drama and that is some serious drama there. You'll have to tell Jay 'no thanks' for me."

Miranda's face fell and she dropped the red jacket she'd been holding up in the mirror. "Pagan, please. This is important to me. Nathan is, he is like, I just haven't felt about anyone like this since, well, since—" I saw tears well up in her eyes as she stared pitifully at me.

"Since Wyatt?" I asked.

She sniffed and nodded. "It isn't as strong as what I felt for Wyatt, but I just met him. He makes my heart race and I get all tingly when he touches me. He isn't Wyatt. No one will ever be Wyatt. But when I'm with him, my heart doesn't hurt."

Well, crap. She finally finds a guy to move on with and he is a friend of my ex. Just freaking perfect.

"I'm sure Nathan will still want to date you even if I don't go out with Jay," I assured her.

Miranda walked over and pushed the clothes beside me out of her way and sat down. "I am sure he would. But I don't know him that well. We just met. We had coffee today and ended up talking for hours. He kissed me. It was…wow. I just want to have you there with me on our first official date. I'll feel better knowing I'm not alone."

Double crap.

"What about Jay's girlfriend?" Please tell me she was a psycho and she might come after my head if I went anywhere with him. This would be my only way out.

"Nathan said that Jay and Victoria aren't an item. She is in the sorority that does things with their fraternity. She has been after him for over a year. Jay puts up with her clinginess, but until he saw you walk into the club he hadn't had a problem with it. Now he is putting a halt to things with Victoria. Nathan said you are all he's talked about since he saw you. Come on, it'll be fun. I need you there."

This was trouble. I looked at Miranda's pleading eyes and knew I wouldn't be able to tell her no. "What time are they going to be here?" I asked and she jumped up and squealed.

"At seven," she replied. It was only three. What was she doing getting ready now?

"We have four hours. Why the clothing panic?"

Miranda rolled her eyes, "Because it's gonna take me four hours to do all that I have to do to be presentable."

I gathered the clothes up that she'd left on my bed and took them over to hers and dropped them. "You put the clothes away. I'm taking a nap. If I have to do this, then I definitely need some sleep. I'm exhausted."

"Fine. I'll find you something to wear. But promise me you'll get up in plenty of time to shower and shave your legs. I'm going to pick you out a mini. Jay always liked your legs."

Ugh.

Dank

A teenage girl not paying attention to a stop sign. It was all too familiar. The difference was I hadn't been stalking this soul. She hadn't intrigued me. The crumpled car was wrapped around an electricity pole. Her parents stood over to the side crying as the desperate hope in their eyes stayed focused on the car. They wanted there to be some chance that their daughter had made it. That when the Jaws of Life pulled the car free, they'd find her alive inside. I knew she wasn't. Her soul was releasing as it sensed my presence.

I reached into the rubble and drew her soul out. It came willingly. The confused look on her face as she looked back at herself and then toward her parents was one I saw daily. She didn't understand just yet that she was no longer in the body.

"Come on, Chick, time for you to head up. You'll have another life before you know it. Say your goodbyes to this one," Gee informed her as she grabbed her hand and they left.

I didn't stay around and wait for her parents to figure out their worst fears were true. I'd had enough of that for one day. I just wanted to go see Pagan, but I had thousands of souls still left to collect.

I walked toward the truck that had flipped in an attempt to miss the girl's car. I stopped where the paramedics were performing CPR on the driver. As the paramedics worked to save him, his soul, already released from his body, was staring down at his empty shell. Gee appeared beside me and without a word she took his hand telling him he'd get to start over and maybe this time he could keep from getting a beer gut.

Pagan

"It is unfair. Completely un-freakin-fair." Miranda scowled into the mirror she had us standing in front of. "I spent hours getting ready. You spent less than thirty minutes and you still look better."

Miranda was gorgeous. She had styled all her wild ringlets perfectly around her face. The red sleeveless top she'd paired with the silver pencil skirt that stopped way before it hit her knees highlighted every curve she had. Nathan didn't stand a chance. "You seriously are confused. You are hot. Embrace it and let's go," I replied before she could change her clothes again.

"Are you sure? You aren't just saying that, are you?" She was still standing in front of the mirror fidgeting with her shirt and hair.

"I am positive. Come on. They are probably already down there waiting for us." And I wanted to get this over with.

"Maybe I should have gone with boots. You look killer in those leather boots," Miranda replied without moving.

I glanced down at the tan leather knee high boots I'd put on with the blue denim mini skirt Miranda had made me wear. "You can wear the boots if you want to. I don't care. I'll go find some other shoes to put on."

Miranda scowled. "No. Those boots won't match what I'm wearing. Besides, you'd end up putting on your Converses or something ridiculous like that. It is a miracle I managed to get you in those. I'm not messing up my luck now."

I smiled because she was correct. If I took these boots off, I would slip on my Converses. "Then, let's go," I replied, and opened the door.

"Okay. Fine. Okay. I can do this," Miranda reminded herself in the mirror, then turned and headed my way. Maybe I'd get her out of here before midnight.

"It's okay, Miranda. He's just a boy and this is just a date," I assured her as I pushed her out the door and into the hallway.

She nodded, "You're right. He's just a boy. It's just a date."

We made our way down to the great room where they'd said they would meet us. I could hear feminine laughter and deep voices as we got closer. "I hear them," Miranda whispered.

"Yep. Seems like they are entertaining some of our neighbors," I replied. Maybe Jay would see someone he liked and leave me alone. Then *she* could deal with crazy Victoria.

We stepped into the room and Jay was talking and laughing with a girl I hadn't met yet, but I'd seen her yesterday when we moved in. Girls always flirted with Jay. He had that friendly kind of personality. Nathan's eyes zoned in on Miranda instantly. The smile on his face as he looked at her made this all worth it. I liked that guy. I just might approve.

Nathan elbowed Jay as we approached and he stopped talking to the redhead and turned to look at us. His eyes swept over me slowly. The girl he'd been talking to reached out and squeezed his arm and said something about seeing him tomorrow night. I almost laughed. He'd just been caught making a date with another girl while waiting for me. That was priceless. If I weren't going on this date for Miranda's sake, I'd use this as my excuse and back out now. I couldn't do that to her though. Not when Nathan had the look of awed worship in his eyes as he stared at her. Yeah, I'd have to deal with Jay the Romeo all night. Maybe Miranda and the redhead could meet and they could double date next time.

"Pagan, wow. You look amazing," Jay said as he stepped toward me, leaving his new friend behind.

"Please don't let me interrupt you," I replied, turning my attention to the girl left waiting on his response.

He was nervous. I smiled at him reassuringly. "Really, Jay. I don't mind. Finish your conversation. I'm in no hurry."

Jay studied me a moment and I could see the indecision on his face. I wasn't the lovesick seventeen-year-old he'd left behind. That ship had sailed. He shook his head and closed the distance between us and rested his hand on my lower back. "I'm ready to go. I was just being friendly."

The frown on the girl's face said otherwise. I moved his hand from my back and took a step back. "If you were asking her out, then please go finish what you started. You're being rude," I whispered.

He let out a sigh. "Fuck."

I watched him as he ran a hand through his hair in frustration. I knew him too well. I could read his body language. "You weren't supposed to hear that. Dammit. I've screwed this up. Asking her out while waiting on you was disrespectful. I'm sorry."

I shrugged, "I'm just on this date because Miranda begged me. You know I can't tell her no. So, no worries. I'd say you could take the redhead instead of me, but Miranda needs me tonight. So, you're stuck with me."

Jay's eyes went wide, "Wait. No. I don't want to be on a date with anyone else. I want to be with you. I've missed you. That back there was just me being a dick. I'm used to asking girls out whenever one seems fun. But it's a habit. I would turn her and anyone else down if I had a chance at going out with you instead."

Well, that was sweet, but it was unfortunate. Because, habit or not, I wasn't stupid enough to go there. "That habit of yours isn't a healthy one and it's mean. Go finish what you started. I'll wait with Miranda and Nathan." I replied and walked toward the door where Miranda and Nathan had gone to give us some privacy. Not that we needed it.

"Sorry for the hold up. Once he is finished finalizing his date for tomorrow night, we'll go."

Nathan closed his eyes and shook his head. "Stupid," he mumbled. When he opened them back up, he looked at me apologetically. "I'm sorry about that. He is a major flirt. But I guess you know that."

Actually, I didn't. Back in high school he hadn't flirted with anyone but me.

"The Jay I knew would have never done that. It pisses me off. I wish you'd flip him off and go back upstairs. Maybe call up Dank Walker since he's hot after your bod and wow him with your sexy ass." Miranda was mad. Jay was in for it.

"You know Dank Walker?" Nathan asked. "As in Cold Soul's lead singer?" I could hear the disbelief in his voice.

"Yep, she knows him. I saw him carrying her books to class today." Miranda replied smugly. I hadn't realized she'd seen that.

"Okay, I'm ready. Again, I'm sorry about that." Jay said as he came up beside us.

"You're a dick," Nathan replied. "A stupid dick."

Jay let out a frustrated sigh, "Yeah, I know."

CHAPTER SEVEN

Pagan

If Jay apologized one more time, I was going to cram a breadstick down his throat. At least then he would shut up. I'd tried to change the subject several times and when that didn't work, I'd started joining in on Miranda and Nathan's conversation. Which worked out well for a while, but now they were huddled together whispering on their side of the large booth and we were on our side with my purse between us as a barrier.

"Are you going to forgive me?" Jay asked.

"I am not mad, Jay. There is nothing to forgive. I'm on this date for Miranda. I never agreed to it because I wanted to spend time with you. So, please, let's talk about something else." I was a broken record.

"So this disinterest I'm getting from you is not because I was a jackass, but because you really didn't care about seeing me to begin with?" he asked with a small amount of surprise in his tone.

"Exactly. You're an old friend. It was nice to see you the other night, but that is about it. I'm here for Miranda."

Jay leaned back in his seat and fiddled with the napkin on his plate. "I had one shot to change your mind and I screwed that up." He was pouting. Fantastic.

"We had our thing. It is a really good memory, but now we're older. Things change."

"You taking my breath away when you walk into a room hasn't changed," he replied when he lifted his eyes to look back at me.

That might just be sweet enough to get him out of trouble if I was interested. But he was just a good friend. I reached over and squeezed his hand. "Thank you. That was nice to hear. But can we just agree to be friends? That way when your habit of asking attractive girls out gets in the way, we can laugh about it," I teased.

Jay gave me a crooked grin. "God, I've missed you."

"Well, I haven't really missed you all that much," I replied, then burst into laughter at the hurt look on his face. "I'm joking. I missed you too." Maybe. When I thought about him. Which hadn't been much over the past year.

"Have you two made up over there? Because if I hear Jay apologize one more time, I may shove him into oncoming traffic," Nathan said from across the table.

"Yes, all is well. We are going to be friends and Jay can ask out anyone he wants to, whenever he wants to." I replied. Nathan studied Jay for a moment with a concerned look on his face, then forced a smile.

"If y'all are okay with that set up, then we are too."

Miranda nodded, "Yep. Sounds like a good plan. Besides, Pagan has a date with Dank Walker Friday night. He gave her backstage passes to his concert. And he's letting me in too."

"How did you know about that?" I hadn't said anything to her about it yet.

She shrugged, "Gee told me."

Figures. Gee was making sure I came. She'd already figured out Miranda got me to do things I didn't want to. After tonight, though, I really did want to go. Dank Walker didn't seem like such a bad decision after being out with a "normal, nice" guy. At least when I was with Dank, he acted like I was the only person around.

"Did you just meet him last night at the club?" Jay asked with a scowl on his face.

"No. He picked up her shoes when we got here yesterday. She dropped a whole box of shoes in the street. He got off his big bad motorcycle and came, picked them up and carried them to her room. I think he's stalking her." Miranda wiggled her eyebrows.

"His band isn't known for their good reputation. They are rowdy and they get into trouble. Hanging around him isn't safe, Pagan." Jay didn't sound convincing.

"So far he's been nothing but nice, polite, and very attentive," I replied as I scooted out of my seat. I wasn't going to be put in a position of defending Dank to Jay. That was ridiculous.

"The important thing here is my best friend is dating the lead singer of Cold Soul and I have backstage passes. Let's not get off topic," Miranda chimed in. Nathan didn't look really thrilled with this either. Now, both of them were scowling. A little jealousy would be good for Nathan. Miranda was making it seem too easy.

"Why did he give you tickets backstage?" Nathan asked as he reached for Miranda's hand.

"Because he knew Pagan wouldn't go without me," she replied. She was also very right. I wouldn't brave that scene if she wasn't beside me.

"Hmmm," was Nathan's only response. Poor guy. He wanted to protest and knew he had no right because he'd just met her.

"So, what movie are we going to see?" I asked to change the subject.

"Well, I was gonna suggest an action movie since there are several out I'd like to see, but after hearing that y'all are gonna be hanging out with a rock band later this week, I feel the need to step up my game. So whatever romance you want to see, I'm willing," Nathan replied.

Miranda laughed, "Oh, you're in luck. I've seen the only romance out right now. It sucked."

"Thank God," Jay sighed dramatically.

"Action movie it is then," Nathan announced.

Dank

I sat on the edge of Pagan's bed and glanced at the clock for the hundredth time in the span of ten minutes. "How long has she been gone?" I asked Gee as she walked into the room.

"I was with you, remember?"

She had been, but she'd headed home before me. I'd started worrying about Pagan with neither of us watching over her.

"Before you point out that I got back an hour before you, I might as well tell you I made a quick stop along the way. I checked in on Pagan's mom and did a sweep to see if I felt the little Voodoo bitch around here anywhere. He's gone. Her mom is good."

I couldn't get mad at her for that.

"She's with him."

Gee only nodded. She and I both knew this had to happen. I couldn't stop it. Her heart had to choose. But, damn, it was hard. Today, she'd melted against me the way she used to. She hadn't pushed me away; she'd wanted me. I know that part of her remembers. Her body responded to me. I had to believe her heart was strong enough to restore her memory. The warmth of her soul's presence washed over me.

"She's back," I said standing up. She'd entered the building.

"I'll see what I can find out. But behave yourself in the corner," Gee replied, waving me away. I wasn't visible to humans in this form. I backed away to stand in the far corner of her room and waited.

The door swung open and Miranda came in chatting happily. I couldn't understand what she was saying because all I could focus on was the high-heeled boots and short skirt Pagan was wearing. *Hell*. I was burning those as soon as she got them off her body. She could cause wars the way she was dressed. I was going to hunt him down and kill him if he touched her. I'd take his sorry soul whether it was time or not.

Gee cleared her throat and I tore my gaze off Pagan's deliciously dressed body to glare at Gee. She must have read the intent on my face; she gave me a warning look. Those boots would be going missing. The skirt too.

"It wasn't so bad, now, was it?" Miranda asked, smiling over at Pagan.

Pagan rolled her eyes and unzipped her boots. Maybe I wouldn't burn them after all. I'd hide them instead. See if I could get her to take them off for me sometime.

"You rocked Jay's world. When did he get so full of himself? Geez. Love the fact that you told him you couldn't care less that he asked that tramp out. And what was up with that? I mean, he was here to pick you up and she was hitting on him. Desperate much?"

Pagan pulled the boot off slowly and if I could drool, I was pretty sure I was. Damn, that was hot. She reached for the other boot to do the same thing.

"I don't care. She can have him. Why did I date the guy for three years? I don't see the appeal."

Her words broke into my lustful imagination and I snapped my head up to look at her face. She didn't like him? What? He was her soul mate.

"He's different from what I remember. He was boring."

Gee smirked in my direction. Pagan reached for the button on her shirt. Oh, yeah.

Then the bathroom door opened and out came a very visible Gee. "So, you bitches have fun?" she asked, interrupting Pagan's shirt unbuttoning. Dammit, Gee.

"Miranda had a wonderful time. I suffered through and Miranda owes me big time."

She really didn't enjoy it…and then she was unbuttoning her shirt again.

"Jay wasn't that bad. He just started the night off by asking another girl out while waiting on Pagan to arrive. We walked in on it. Pagan handled it brilliantly and comically, but he still looked like an ass."

Jay had asked someone else out? Did the guy not see what Pagan was wearing? Damn. I might not have to worry about this at all. He was an idiot. The last button on Pagan's shirt came undone and she dropped it to the floor. I moved so that I could sink down on the bed and watch.

"She's excited about Friday night. She won't admit it, but I can tell," Miranda said, picking up Pagan's discarded shirt and throwing it at her.

"You change your mind about guys in a band?" Gee asked. I wasn't sure what she meant, but I'd ask her as soon as she got out of here.

Pagan lifted one shoulder and I prayed by all that was holy that she'd take off that pink bra. This may be invading her privacy, but I was Death, dammit. I should get some privileges. "I decided to not judge a book by its cover. Can't hurt to give Dank Walker a chance."

"He may want more than a chance," Gee murmured for my ears only.

Pagan began to unbutton her skirt. Yes, please.

"I'm gonna go shower. Y'all feel free to talk about me because I know you will," Pagan informed them and walked into the bathroom just before her skirt slid down her legs and hit the floor. I was tempted to follow her in there, but that would be wrong. She would be furious if she knew. I glanced over at Gee who looked ready to crack up laughing at me.

CHAPTER EIGHT

Pagan

"I stay out of sight and only whisper to you.
Words I can't say. Words you don't need to hear. Words I can't keep from
tangling my way.
Now, I can't stand alone. I can't ignore what I've been shown.
You've claimed me and I don't care who knows. You've claimed me and
I don't care if it shows.
I'm weakened and I'm strengthened in your arms.
You've claimed me and I need to feel you close.

You stand wanting more than you could ever understand.
I stand helpless, needing to give in to your every command. Wanting to
see you smile has consumed me and tied both my hands.
Nothing I offer could ever be worthy of your love.
It's a miracle that you saw me and never ran.
I will spend my whole life trying to be the man you think I am.
Now, I can't stand alone. Now, I am under your influence. I can't ignore
what I've been shown.
You've claimed me and I don't care who knows.
You've claimed me and I don't care if it shows.
I'm weakened and I'm strengthened in your arms. You've claimed me and
I need to feel you close.

You hold fire within your gaze.
It mesmerizes everyone you allow into your maze. I know nothing of your
thoughts, but I need to bask within the warmth of your rays. Nothing you do
could ever be wrong. You're forever perfect in every way.
Now, I can't stand alone. Now, I am under your influence.
You've taken over me and now, I can't ignore what I've been shown. You've
claimed me and I don't care who knows. You've claimed me and I don't care
if it shows. I'm weakened and I'm strengthened in your arms.
You've claimed me and I need to feel you close."

The hauntingly sweet music played over and over again in the darkness.
I couldn't open my eyes, but I wasn't scared. I knew I was safe. The words
soothed me and eventually I fell back into a deep sleep. Bright blue eyes
that glowed against the night were the last things I remembered.

"*Get up!* You are like the sleeping dead, I swear. Get your lazy ass up.
We have class in ten minutes," Miranda was yelling at me while pelting
me with her pillow.

I groaned, rolled over, and blocked the onslaught of her feather pillow.
"I'm awake. You can stop now."

"It's about time. I tried everything else. I've been awake for over an
hour. Your stupid alarm clock made sure I woke up. How you slept through
that annoying beeping is beyond me."

"I slept through the alarm clock?" I asked sitting up and squinting my
eyes from the sun's rays. It was after eight o'clock. I wasn't going to make
it to my Literature class on time. Crap. Great first impression.

"Yeah, you did. That's like happened…never. What did you do, take
a sleeping pill?"

I stood up and stretched. "No, I just slept really good," I paused and
thought about the strange darkness and the music. The voice and the
song. "There was this song," I said, then stopped. Miranda would think
I'd lost my mind.

"No time to talk about songs right now. Here, throw this on and go brush your stinky teeth. We gotta go. Good thing you look hot without makeup."

Miranda shoved a pair of shorts and a shirt into my arms and pushed me into the bathroom. I guess I wouldn't tell her about my song. Although, I wanted to tell someone.

* * * *

Dank wasn't in literature class. I was disappointed he hadn't shown up and carried my books, but relieved because I could focus on my work. Being able to listen and focus was a good thing in college. Day one and we already had an assignment. We also had to work in groups. Not my thing. Three girls and three guys per group. We had to read three different works of literature about self-destructive men. Then, we had to write a female point of view paper and a male point of view paper on how exactly the males in the assigned stories were self-destructive. We also had to identify who we could relate them to in today's society and describe how this self-destruction affected politics.

I shoved my books into my bag and headed to the board to read the group assignments. Each person in our group had an email address beside their name so that we could contact each other once we'd read the first book, *Ethan Frome*. I was a step ahead. I'd already read it. The line was dwindling because several people left without looking. I walked up and scanned the list for my name.

Keith Fromer
Pagan Moore
Jessi Gilheart
Jackson Driver
Maddy McGowin
Dank Walker

I stopped reading the names and glanced behind me. How was Dank's name on here? He wasn't in this class. Was he? The girl behind me cleared her throat in an irritated manner. I took a quick picture of the list of the people in my group and their email addresses with my iPhone and moved out of the way.

Had Dank skipped class?

Dank

By the time I was finished with souls, I was too late to go to literature class with Pagan. I hated I'd missed an opportunity to sit by her, but I'd stayed late last night to sing her to sleep. That was something I missed. I couldn't bring myself to leave until I knew she was sleeping peacefully.

The doors to the English building opened and Pagan came walking out with a frown on her face. I didn't like for her to be unhappy. I walked out of my hiding spot and into her path.

"Oh! Dank. You're here." She seemed surprised.

"Yeah. Were you hoping I'd dropped out?" I asked teasingly.

Her frown faded and she beamed up at me. That was better. "I was curious as to why you missed your first day of literature."

She'd seen the list. We'd be spending study time together too. The more time I could get with her the better. Now that I knew she wasn't really impressed with Jay, I could breathe a little easier.

"I was out late. I'll catch up."

"I've got notes. I have some time before I meet Miranda. If you want to go get some coffee or just go over to a picnic table, I could give you everything that you missed," she offered.

I would have preferred we go somewhere more private, but that wasn't a possibility. I'd never be able to explain how it was I could sneak into her room so easily and I didn't have a room for her to sneak into.

That was something I really needed to rectify. I needed a place to at least appear as if I lived there. She was going to be curious and until I knew she loved me, I couldn't tell her who I really was. I didn't think she'd accept me if I explained my existence any sooner.

The library. It could be secluded if you went to the right places. "What about the library?" I asked. Her eyes lit up.

"Perfect. We need to get you a copy of *Ethan Frome* if you haven't already read it."

We could pretend I needed the copy of Ethan Frome. "Let's go get that book," I replied.

Pagan nodded and started to walk toward the library. I took her book bag. I hated seeing her carry it around. It looked so heavy on her shoulders. "I got this. Lead the way." I told her when she looked back at me. She blushed and mumbled a thank you as she headed toward the large stone three-story building that I knew had a very quiet and secluded top floor. I'd checked it out already.

I opened one of the large double doors and let Pagan walk inside. "Go to the top floor," I whispered to her and nodded toward the staircase to our left.

Pagan didn't argue. She did as instructed and I followed behind her. The view of her cute little bottom in the shorts she had on today was making this idea better by the minute. She reached the top floor and glanced back at me. "Where to?"

"There is a study area in the back that is usually empty so we can talk without disturbing anyone," I explained.

No one was back here. If they were, I was prepared to convince them to leave.

"Do you have another class today? This was it for me." Pagan asked as she pulled out a chair and sat down.

"I'm done for the day, too, so no need to hurry," I replied. I wanted all the time I could get up here alone with her.

"Okay, good," she smiled and pulled out her literature book and a notebook. "My handwriting can be sloppy when I try to write fast. I'm supposed to be getting a laptop in the mail next week. Mom is sending it to me. Until then, I have to scribble everything down."

She had to go a week without a laptop. I knew it would be difficult for her. I wanted her to have something to type on. Pagan liked to take thorough notes. She wouldn't be able to do that with a pen and paper. "I've got a laptop I'm not using. You're welcome to borrow it until yours gets here."

Her eyes lit up, "Really? You have an extra?"

I didn't own a laptop, but I'd go purchase one as soon as I left here. "It's all yours."

"Thank you. You're a life-saver. That is such a sweet offer. I promise I'll take care of it."

The look on her face made me want to go buy her five laptops and anything else she wanted.

"About the concert Friday night," she began. Please don't let her be backing out on me now. I wanted her there. "What time do we need to be there? Do you go early and warm up?"

"Concert starts at eight, but we'll warm up around five. Then we relax and hang out backstage until show time."

"Oh, wow. What time should we get there?"

I hadn't been prepared for this question just yet. I'd wanted to ease her into coming to my practice with me, and letting Miranda come with Gee later.

"Would you be against riding with me to practice and staying the entire evening with me?"

She didn't respond right away. I watched as a series of emotions crossed her face. "Um, well. What about Miranda and Gee? Would they be coming early too?"

I shook my head, "No, they'd come a little later."

I wanted her without her posse.

"Oh," she replied and bit her bottom lip several times before looking back up at me. "Would it be okay if I just came with them? Miranda is looking forward to this and Gee still makes her nervous. Plus, while you're warming up, I'll be all alone."

I tried hard not to let the disappointment show on my face. "That's fine, Pagan. Whatever makes you feel comfortable." Reminding myself that this was going to take time was difficult. I wanted to get back what we had. But to Pagan I was still a guy she'd just met. One she wasn't sure she trusted.

"Okay, thank you," she replied and began pulling more papers out of her book bag. I'd forgotten we were here to catch me up on what I missed in class. "Like I said, I took notes, but I probably took more than necessary. You can look over them and write down the highlights. I'm going to go find a copier and make you a copy of the syllabus. Oh, and I'll look for the book, too." She stood up and headed for the stairs. I leaned back in my chair and closed my eyes. One day, I'd have her back.

CHAPTER NINE

Pagan

Finding the copier was easier than I'd thought. Finding *Ethan Frome* was also a breeze. Seven minutes later, I was headed back upstairs to the little secluded hideaway with Dank. I had used finding the copier and book as an excuse to get away from him so I could take a deep breath and gather my thoughts. He was definitely interested in me. I couldn't deny that now. I was also more than positive he'd picked this area for more than study purposes and it excited me and scared me all at same time.

Dank was leaning back in his chair with his feet propped up on the table and crossed at the ankles. Something about that pose was oddly familiar. This was the second time today I felt like I'd seen him doing something similar before. Was I dreaming about him? Was that it?

"That was fast," Dank drawled as he turned his head and his blue eyes met mine.

I placed the book in front of him and walked back over to my empty chair. "Here you go," I handed him the syllabus. "You are all set. Did you look over my notes?" I asked to make small talk.

Dank let his legs drop back down to the floor and he leaned forward on the table, "Yeah. I got what I needed. Thank you for helping me get set up. I shouldn't have missed this morning."

When he dropped his voice like that, I wanted to fan myself. He was already lethally sexy. He didn't have to make his voice go all husky and deep. It made the sexy worse.

"I'm glad you're coming Friday night," he said leaning closer to me. I felt myself leaning toward him, unable to stop the pull.

"Thank you for inviting me," I replied. My voice sounded breathless. Just great. I sounded as affected as I felt.

Dank pushed his chair back and stood up. I watched as he walked over toward me, then held out his hand to me. I knew what he wanted and I wanted it too. If I was going to get a re-enactment of what happened yesterday by the tree, then I was very okay with this.

Dank pulled me up and wrapped my hand back behind his neck. I threaded my fingers through his hair and he closed his eyes and took a deep breath. I liked seeing how my touch affected him like that. Slipping my other hand up his arm and around his neck, I watched his face, fascinated by the eagerness evident in the tight way he held his mouth and the gleam in his eyes.

I decided I wouldn't wait for him this time. I pulled him to me and captured his mouth with mine, unable to resist licking his bottom lip as I kissed him. It was so full and soft looking that I'd wanted a taste of it ever since the first time I'd seen him, whether I wanted to admit it or not.

Dank's hands slid up my ribs until they rested just below the underside of my bra. As far as knowing about boys, I was pretty naive. Jay and I had done some kissing and rubbing, but nothing too exciting. I was more than positive that if Dank touched my breasts, I would burst into flames. There was no way he didn't notice my rapid breathing. I was almost embarrassed by my reaction to his touch, but the soft appreciative growls coming from his chest as he tasted my lips and my skin assured me he was enjoying this just as much as I was.

"Please, ride with me Friday night," Dank begged as he continued kissing down my neck and along my collarbone. This was an unfair request. He got me all hot and bothered, then begged me. How was a girl supposed to think clearly?

"I can't. Miranda needs me," I replied, my heart slamming against my chest. His mouth hovered over the low neckline of my shirt and his warm breath tickled the sensitive skin there. I was almost at the point of begging when his hands slid down and cupped my butt, picked me up and sat me on the table behind me. Dank stepped between my legs and put his hands back on my waistline.

"It's probably for the best," he finally said as his mouth lowered to cover mine again. I wanted to know what he meant by that, but his tongue was inside my mouth doing things to me I'd never had done before. I pulled his body closer to mine and kissed him back with all the excitement and need he was provoking in me.

"If you come, I won't be able to practice. I'd want to be alone with you. Listening to you talk, watching you smile, finding reasons to kiss your body."

Whoa. Maybe I should go…

His hands slowly slid up my stomach until they were gently cupping my breasts. When the pads of his thumbs grazed my nipples, I broke free from the kiss and gasped for air. The sensation coming from his touch shot through my body straight to my core.

Dank stilled and watched me. He didn't move his thumbs again, but he didn't move his hands away either. I gazed up at him letting him see I was waiting. He'd surprised me, but I wanted more of this. His thumbs moved again and this time his hands shifted until his fingers were slipping into my bra and tugging it down.

That's when we heard the footsteps and voices on the stairs. Dank's hands were gone instantly and he was straightening my shirt as he backed away from me. I scrambled off the table and sat back in my chair because I wasn't sure my legs were ready to actually walk just yet.

I braved a glimpse at Dank who was sitting back in his chair with my notes in his hands. His mouth was fixed in a crooked grin and I could see traces of my lip gloss on his lips. Reaching over, I ran my thumb over his lips to wipe away the traces of our kiss. Dank grabbed my wrist and kissed it before letting it go and standing up.

"I can't stay in here and look at you without touching you. I need some fresh air," he admitted.

I liked that. I liked that a lot.

Dank

My concentration was shot to hell. All I could think about was the way Pagan had felt in my hands, all soft and sweet. If we hadn't been interrupted, I wasn't sure how much further she'd have let me go and if I'd have been able to stop if she didn't stop me first.

I would be leaving to gather souls soon, but first, I had a band practice. I didn't show up for all the practices, but luckily, the band members never remembered that. Sometimes they were too high; other times I had to help them forget.

"You practicing tonight?" Gee asked as she appeared in front of my Harley after I'd parked it.

"Yeah, why? Is Pagan okay?" I asked not getting off in case I needed to leave.

Gee rolled her eyes and shook her head, "Pagan is fine. She's holed up in her room studying. I've been banned from entering. Apparently, I interrupt her."

Smiling, I got off my bike and headed for the entrance to the club we used for practice. They had a back room with a smaller stage that was a good set up. The drummer, Loose, was related to the owner. Gee fell into step beside me.

"What are you doing?" I asked glancing over at her.

"I'm bored. And Loose is sexy as hell."

Great. Not what I needed. Gee hooking up with a human. The Deity would be all over me. "You can't do anything with him, Gee. He's human."

"It ain't like I'm gonna marry him and have his damn babies, Dank. The guy's a man whore. A sexy dirty boy who appeals to me. Just a night of fun is all I want."

I stopped outside the entrance and put my hand on the door to keep her from opening it. "You can't go in there and flirt with him. I have the Deity screwing with me right now because I pissed them off. If you break the same rule, it will be me who suffers."

Gee rolled her eyes, "Drama much? I just want to have a little kinky fun with him. That has never been a rule breaker. It's the falling in love with humans that is a no-no. Fucking the naughty ones isn't a big deal. It's been done before."

I couldn't argue with her because she was right. As long as she wasn't going to fall in love with Loose, we'd be safe. And I knew Loose was in no danger of falling in love with any one female because he loved them all.

Gee walked in front of me into the practice room and I realized she'd done a quick clothing change. The jeans and "Fuck You" tee shirt she had been wearing were now gone and she was in a short tight red dress with black boots that had red skulls on the sides. Shaking my head, I headed over to the cooler and grabbed a bottle of water.

"Look at you. Thank you, all that is holy, for the tits about to fall out of that dress," Loose called from behind the drums.

"Down, boy. We have to run through Friday night's songs before you haul her off to the restroom and make use of your favorite stall," Les, the other singer and bass guitar, warned him.

"Dank just got here. Why don't y'all do your warm up thing while I keep his friend company. You are sharing, aren't you, Dank?" Loose asked.

I silently cursed Gee before turning around to face the band. "She's all yours," I replied.

Loose was off his stool and jumping off the stage in seconds. "I'll be back," he called out as he slipped a hand over Gee's ass. When he lowered his head to her ear to start whispering, I blocked them out. I did not want to hear that. The boy had just met his match. He'd never be the same after this.

"You okay letting him take your girl like that? 'Cause I don't want no fighting before a gig as big as the one on Friday night," Les said as he walked over to get a bottle of water.

"She isn't my girl, just an old friend. If she were my girl, he wouldn't have walked out of here alive."

Les nodded and took a swig. "Noted. You want to go ahead and run through cords while Loose entertains himself and we wait on the other two to get here?"

"Yeah, let's get this done."

CHAPTER TEN

Pagan

Only my Literature and Science professors felt the need to start classes a week ahead of time. The rest of my classes didn't begin until next week. We were welcome to go meet the professors and pick up our syllabuses, so after I'd done that, my first week of college classes was over.

I could reread *Ethan Frome* since it had been two years since I had read it. I could also go get coffee and go over my Calculus syllabus. Calculus scared the hell out of me; I was not a math person and never had been.

Miranda walked out of the bathroom dressed like she was going out clubbing, but it was only one in the afternoon. "How do I look?" she asked twirling around.

"Like you want to dance the night away and have free drinks brought to you all night long," I replied.

Miranda grinned, "Good. Because I do."

"Wait. What? You do realize it's just one o'clock? Clubs don't open until eight and without Gee you're never getting in."

Miranda shrugged and began posing in the mirror. "Not going to a club. I'm going to my very first frat party."

"At one in the afternoon?"

Miranda gave me an exasperated look, then looked back into the mirror and puckered her lips. "No, silly. Nathan will be here to pick me up at six. We are going to get something to eat, then head to the ATO house."

She still wasn't making sense. "Then why are you ready five hours early?"

Miranda stopped doing sexy poses in the mirror and turned around and looked at me. "This is a trial run. I have a couple more to do before he gets here. I'm seeing how I look like this. Then I'm going to change and pull my hair up and maybe use a little blue eye shadow—or do you think that is too much? Maybe I should go with the silver." She continued to ramble and I covered my face with a pillow. I was exhausted just thinking about getting ready once, much less several times in a row.

"I think you are officially insane," I replied.

Miranda laughed, "I know you do. But I have to be perfect. This night has to be perfect. I really like him, Pagan."

I was glad she did, but honestly, did she have to play real life Barbie doll in order to impress him?

A knock on the door interrupted us and I moved the pillow from my face and sat up. Miranda walked to the door and opened it up without asking who it was first. When I saw who was standing there, I really wish she had. It was Victoria.

"Can I help you?" Miranda asked when she recognized her. She stepped in front of Victoria and put her hand on her hip. She was doing her protective stance. Like Miranda was big enough to take down anyone.

"I'm here to see your friend," Victoria replied.

"This is not your day then, 'cause that ain't gonna happen."

I could hear the snarl in her voice. Miranda had just made an enemy. "You do know that Nathan is screwing my Kappa sister Siera? They've been fuck-buddies now for over three months. He was with her last night after he left you."

I was off the bed and moving Miranda out of the way before the bitch could say any more. I didn't believe her, but I knew Miranda did. I was good with reading people and I had seen the way Nathan looked at Miranda. I didn't doubt he had once been messing around with this Siera, but I didn't think for a minute that he still was.

"You came here for me. What do you want?" I demanded, wishing I had kept my distance from Jay. This was the kind of drama I hated and avoided at all costs. I was not into cat fights—especially over a guy I didn't want.

"Whatever you think you and Jay are going to rekindle, you need to think again. Back the hell off, bitch! I'm not sharing. He is in my bed most nights. You're just a new flavor. He gets bored with them fast." The venom dripping from her tone was really uncalled for. She was upset over nothing.

"I hope you and Jay have a long happy life in bed together. I don't care. I'm not interested in him. He's an old friend and nothing more. So take your threats and go share them with the redhead down the hall because she is the only one in the building who wants Jay." I didn't give her time to respond. I slammed the door in her face.

The room was eerily quiet and I looked back to see where Miranda was. The bathroom door was open and the shower was running. This was not a good sign. She had several other outfits and hairstyles to try before six. If she was showering, that meant she believed the spiteful words that spewed from Victoria's mouth.

I walked into the bathroom and pulled myself up and sat down on the counter. I could hear the soft sobs and hiccups coming from the shower.

"For what it's worth, I don't believe her," I said loudly enough she could hear me over the water.

Miranda sniffed and let out a hard laugh. "I do. He wouldn't take me to his apartment last night. Even after I asked. He said we'd do that another night. He got a phone call right after we finished dinner and he acted funny and nervous the rest of the evening. He even cut our date short. I thought I was imagining things. He had been so sweet when he'd kissed me," another sob broke free.

I was ready to go strangle this Nathan guy. "Then he is the biggest idiot known to man. You are gorgeous and funny and any guy who is lucky enough to have you interested in him should realize his supreme luck and not screw it up."

Miranda let out a sad laugh, "I love you, Pagan."

"I love you, too," I replied.

"Could we watch season two of The Vampire Diaries tonight and eat ice cream? I need it. The first time I think I like someone after Wyatt and this happens. It sucks," she hiccupped.

"I'll go get the ice cream. You dig out the DVDs." I told her as I got down from the counter.

"I miss him, Pagan," she sounded so sad and defeated. I didn't have to ask whom she missed. I knew she meant Wyatt. I missed him, too. But I knew her loss was completely different.

"I know. Finish your shower and I'll be back soon with plenty of ice cream and two spoons."

"'Kay."

* * * *

Miranda's phone had finally stopped ringing. Once I'd barred the door and informed Nathan that if he came in, I would call campus security and have him arrested, he'd finally given up and left. That was two days ago. I'd been holed up in our room with Miranda ever since. We'd watched seasons one, two, and three of The Vampire Diaries. We had eaten more gallons of ice cream than should be legal. I doubted I would fit into my jeans on Monday.

I glanced back at the clock. It was after four and I knew Gee would be barging in here any minute now to get us moving. Miranda was better today. She and I had laughed most of the morning. The only thing that had caused her to frown was the ringing of her phone. It had finally stopped sometime around lunch. Either Nathan had given up or he was moving to plan B since plan A sucked. Miranda was not going to answer that phone. Sometime around lunch yesterday, she'd gone from being sad to being angry. She had even barged out of the room saying she was going to get fresh air, go running and maybe flirt with some boys. I felt much better about her recovery.

The door opened and Gee stuck her head in, "You ready to be a sexy-ass groupie tonight? You're VIP, baby," she finished her comment with a wink.

I hadn't seen Dank since the incident with Miranda. He'd called and texted me a few times having gotten my number and permission to call through Gee. Last night he'd even been a little naughty in his texts. I'd secretly gotten a thrill out of it, but he hadn't let it get too far. Before I got hot and bothered, he'd said goodnight and told me to go to bed so I'd be rested for tonight.

"Yeah, I'm ready, but I am not a groupie," I replied.

"You are *so* a groupie. The only kind of groupie that Dank Walker will let get near him."

CHAPTER ELEVEN

Dank

The rest of the band had crashed in the main lounge area backstage. I liked them enough, but generally before a gig, they had groupies with them and they got on my nerves. I could smell the sadness and depravity on many of them. What human men saw as sexy often repelled me because all I could see was the soul. Their souls were weak and damaged.

I sank down on the leather sofa and propped my feet up. Pagan would be here any minute, along with Gee and Miranda who would want to meet the rest of the band. Miranda was going to be disappointed. They were just like any other rock band. They had their addictions. They thought all females worshiped them. They were everything Pagan feared I was.

A knock at the door surprised me. I figured Gee would walk right in.

"Come in," I called out and stood up to go greet Pagan. I wanted to show her around. But it wasn't Pagan. It was a groupie I'd seen with Loose earlier. Groupies weren't welcome in here. "You got the wrong room," I replied sitting back down to wait on Pagan's arrival.

"Oops," she giggled and stepped into the room closing the door behind her. Did the girl not speak English? She also had herpes. I could smell it on her body.

"Go. Out. Now." I ordered pointing to the door. I'd be seeing her soul again much sooner than I should if she kept the drug use up.

"Demanding. I like it when a man is the boss," she slurred walking over toward me. Her soul was tarnished. The outward appearance had all the things humans looked for, but the inside was ugly.

"This is your last warning. I'll call security and you'll be thrown out." This happened once or twice a gig. It had become a game to the groupies to see if one of them was talented enough to get me to let them stay. They didn't understand that what I saw wasn't appealing.

"You are a grumpy pants. I was warned before I came in here. I bet I can make you a happy pants," she was almost near me when I moved out of her way and she stumbled forward and landed on the couch. Pulling my phone from my pocket, I dialed the backstage security number.

"I got one in my room that refuses to leave. I want her out of the building."

"On it, Mr. Walker," was the quick reply.

"Oh, poo, you didn't even let me show you how very talented I am," she whined from her sprawled out position on the couch.

The door swung open and in walked Gee followed by Pagan and Miranda. At least I was on the other side of the room from the half dressed girl laying out on the couch like she was waiting on me.

"Do I need to call security?" Gee asked as she looked over at the girl whose damaged soul was also the only thing Gee saw.

"Already did. I'm waiting on him to come pick her up." I replied stepping around her to reach out and take Pagan's hand.

Before her memory loss, Pagan had seen this before. During the time my fans knew I had a girlfriend, it had gotten worse. We made a game out of it. Pagan would guess how many girls we'd have break into my room before the show. Now, she just looked concerned.

"I've been waiting for you," I assured her as she took in the girl whose shirt was missing and her very large fake boobs spilled out of the bra she was wearing. It did look incriminating. "She'll be gone in a second. Security is coming to get her, she came in uninvited."

Pagan frowned and turned her gaze to me, "Where is her shirt?" she asked slowly as if waiting on me to admit I had something to do with her lack of proper clothing.

"Probably in the other room where the band is. She came in here like that. My refusal to hang out with the band and groupies often sends the braver ones in here to see if they can change my mind. They can't. I don't do drugs and STDs."

A small smile tugged on Pagan's lips as the door opened and one of the guys on the club's security team walked in and hauled the girl up from her spot on the couch. "I want her gone from the club while I'm here," I reminded him.

He nodded, "Yes, sir."

"Why do they get to stay? They came in uninvited, too," she whined and slapped at the guy's back. "Leave me alone. I have bigger tits than they do and I'll suck," the door slammed behind them cutting off whatever else she was about to say. Thank Deity.

Once the door closed, I took a deep breath.

"Wow, that was interesting," Pagan teased.

I grinned at her, then shifted my attention to Gee. "Why don't you take Miranda to meet the rest of the band?" It wasn't a suggestion; I knew Gee and everyone else in the room knew that too.

"Yay!" Miranda clapped her hands. "I brought my Sharpie—will they autograph my shirt?"

She was wearing a white shirt that the band had sold at a beach concert last year. She had taken Pagan with her, even though Pagan didn't know who or what I was. "They'll sign anything you ask them to, but remember they are a raunchy crowd. You'll wind up with a lot of names on your chest."

Miranda beamed at my warning. She was definitely in a better mood. Pagan had told me about what happened with the other girl. I wished I could tell her that it would be okay. That the soul she'd loved in Wyatt was the same soul that was living inside Nathan. But I couldn't. She'd have to figure this out on her own.

"I got this. She'll be fine," Gee replied and led Miranda back out of the door, leaving me alone with Pagan.

"Why do I feel like you just sent them away on purpose?" Pagan asked as she looked up at me through her eyelashes.

"Because you're a smart girl. I have a thing for females with brains," I replied.

"Ooooh, that explains why you weren't attracted to the topless Barbie who was more than willing to do whatever you wanted with her." I cringed mentally thinking of the girl who had been in here. I didn't even want to take Pagan over to the couch and have her sit where the girl had been. It felt tainted now.

"All I wanted to do with her was get her the hell away from me. Nothing about that train wreck was attractive."

Pagan liked my answer. I could see it in her eyes. I was proving to her that I wasn't the depraved sex-crazed man-whore she assumed I was just because I was a singer in a band. She took a step toward me and I didn't reach out and touch her. I wanted to see exactly what she was planning to do. If she started to move, I would have grabbed her and held on, but right now, I wanted her to feel like she was in control.

"That is very sexy, Dank Walker. Just so you know. Most guys wouldn't have cared about anything other than her looks." The awe in her voice made my chest expand.

"I'm glad you realize I'm a little deeper than you first assumed," I replied.

Pagan placed a hand on my chest and ran it up until she was touching the necklace that she'd bought me before my last concert. Before her memory was taken from her. She'd said lead singers needed some jewelry. She'd chosen a Celtic knot on a black string. She said the knot was endless and so were we. I hadn't taken it off since. I kept it tucked inside my shirt unless I was going onstage. I didn't like people touching it. Pagan had given it to me. It was sacred. She held the knot in her hand and I felt an odd sense of power at having her hands on it again.

"It's a Celtic knot. Why did you choose this?" she asked looking up at me with intrigue in her eyes.

"Someone gave it to me," I explained, waiting to see if any of this clicked with her. She ran her thumb over the cool metal.

"The knot is never ending," she said quietly as if she was repeating a memory to herself.

I didn't respond. I didn't want to interrupt any small memory that may have been trying to break through. She dropped her hand from my chest and turned and walked away from me. That wasn't what I was expecting.

"What's wrong?" I asked almost afraid to speak.

She shrugged and I heard a small sniffle. Dammit, she was crying. Why was she crying? I took two long strides until I was standing behind her and I pulled her back against my chest. "Why are you crying?" I asked gently.

She took a deep breath and shook her head, "I don't know." She reached up and wiped away the tears from her cheeks. "I just suddenly wanted to cry. It was weird. I'm sorry. I don't know what's wrong with me."

Hope. I had hope. The Celtic knot was triggering something inside her.

Pagan

Dank was going to think I was an idiot. The lump that had formed in my throat the moment I held the necklace in my hands had been odd. I had to ask about it and he talked about it with such reverence in his voice that I couldn't fight back the sob. My eyes had instantly filled with tears. How crazy was that?

Surprisingly enough, he wasn't calling security to haul me out of here. He was holding me. Was this guy even real? Most guys would have written me off as a lunatic. His arms were tightly wrapped around me. I rested my head back on his chest and enjoyed it. Something was comforting about letting him hold me. I felt safe.

"We go onstage soon. Will you come watch me from the side of the stage? I'd like to be able to look over and see you safely away from the crowd out there. This is one of the wilder clubs we play."

His protective streak should have annoyed me. I had just met the guy…but it didn't. I liked it. Had Jay ever been protective? Had anyone ever been protective of me other than my mother?

"Okay. What about Miranda and Gee?" I asked still standing with my back to his chest and his arms firmly around me.

"They can stay too if they like. They're welcome to walk around or stand with you. Gee knows the out of bounds places."

That was something I wanted answered. Who was Gee to him? "How do you know Gee? I thought the first time I saw you that you two might be a couple, but I've figured out that isn't the case."

Dank turned me around to face him. "Gee is one of the oldest friends I have."

That was a weird way of saying it. Did he mean they'd been friends a long time? Like since they were kids? I opened my mouth to ask, when the door opened and in came guys that looked like I expected guys in a rock band to look like.

"Fuck, man, I was pissed when they told me you threw the blond hottie out, but *dayam*, bro, no wonder you did if she was busting up this shit." A guy with long blond dreadlocks pulled back in a ponytail and dark brown eyes rimmed with red as if he'd had very little sleep or maybe smoked a few too many joints, openly appraised me.

"Loose, this is Pagan. She's with me. Only me," Dank replied, keeping his hands locked on my waist. "No one goes near her. No one touches her."

Loose raised his almost completely shaved off eyebrows, "Got it. No sharing of Dankster's girl. It's a damn shame, though, 'cause she sure is pretty."

A guy with short, spikey, unnaturally red hair shoved Loose. "You're gonna get your ass beat. Back up and shut up. That dude is scary as shit."

Dank pointed toward the guy who just spoke, "That's Les. He has the most normal name out of the group. He's also the other voice."

"Hello," I replied, not sure what else I was supposed to say.

"She's all proper and shit. That's sexy," Loose replied, winking at me.

A guy with a shaved head and at least fifteen piercings per ear walked up and grabbed Loose by the shoulders, "Get your ass on stage before we are minus one drummer."

"That is Rubber and please don't ask," Dank said as the bald guy nodded and shoved Loose out the door.

"Show time, Dank; let's go blow this place up!" Les called out as he followed the other two.

"Were they what you expected?" Dank asked looking at me with a worried frown.

"Yes. Exactly what I expected," I assured him and headed for the door.

"Wait, I forgot to mention something," he said.

I glanced back at him, "What is that?"

He closed the distance I'd put between us. "I need a good luck kiss."

Oh my, yes. I could do that. I placed both my hands on his shoulders and leaned up to kiss him swiftly on the mouth. He had other ideas. He pulled my bottom lip into his mouth and sucked gently before slipping his tongue inside to tangle with mine. It was over too soon. He stepped back and took a deep breath.

"Okay. I gotta get out there before I decide they can do this without me and lock that door."

The giddy feeling from the sexual power that his words gave me was surprising. I really liked that he was so attracted to me. But then again, what female wouldn't?

Dank reached down and took my hand as we walked toward the stage entrance. "With a wink, he let go of my hand and stepped out on stage. The smoke consumed him and I had a moment of panic as the memory of being trapped in smoke and having someone rescue me flashed in my memory—but that had never happened.

The drums began beating a foreign tribal sound, and screaming fans quieted down. I watched as Dank walked out from the smoke and into the red spotlight. Something that looked like panties and a couple of bras were slung up onto the stage. That would take some getting used to. Les stepped out into the light next, and Rubber came in last.

The tribal beat grew louder as Loose played the hypnotic sound. The sound of an electric guitar entered the mix and then Dank's voice joined in.

Danger, Danger running cold
Knowing, but fearing just the same
Death comes and yet you don't let go
Standing while its steel bands hold
Don't walk. Don't walk where light cannot shine
You know the warning has been told
It comes for what is mine and I know it will be so.

Let go, it's all there is that's left. Let go, your sin has no wrath.
Danger was Hell's last request.
Let go, it's all there is that's left. Let go, your sin has no wrath.
Forgiveness wasn't given yet. Not yet. Not yet.
No regrets.

"That is their new one. I love it," Miranda whispered as she came up beside me.

"It's some morbid shit is what it is," Gee said with an annoyed tone.

I watched Dank as he sang the words and wondered what song of his I'd heard before. His voice was familiar. I'd heard him sing something. His stuff wasn't mainstream, so I knew it hadn't been on the radio.

He shifted his eyes to me and a grin tugged at the corners of his mouth before he turned back to the crowd and started the next song. Les talked to their fans. Dank might be the voice, but he wasn't the personality. He didn't perform for the crowd. Les was doing a good job of that. The girls chanted Dank's name just the same.

"He plays that mystery card well," Miranda said approvingly. "They love him because they feel he is hiding some big secret and they want to know it."

Gee snorted and we both turned to look at her. If Dank had a secret, she'd be the one to know it. "No one wants inside his head. Trust me."

I felt the need to defend him. Shaking that off, I looked back out at him. I'd known him one week. She'd known him most of his life. I knew nothing really. "Stop frowning, Peggy Ann. I was only teasing. Dank Walker has his secrets, but nothing you would run from. Trust me when I tell you that."

I was happy she had changed her tone about Dank. Something deep inside me wanted to defend him. It as odd and I had no explanation for it but I felt a pull toward Dank that made no sense.

I started to say something to Miranda when Dank's guitar became the only sound we could hear. The rest of the band had stepped back leaving him at the center of the stage. Something in me ached. Was it the lonely sad sound of the music or just seeing Dank standing there in the darkness all alone? I wasn't sure what it was exactly, but it made my chest hurt. Then he began singing. Each word tugged at me. There was something about that song that got to me. The melody wrapped around me. I wanted to go to him and hold him. I braced myself against the wall as the words "Yet You Stay" caused my heart to race. What was wrong with me? My head pounded violently as the words "Yet You Stay" drummed over and over again inside it and my breathing became difficult. My vision blurred. I heard Gee asking me if I was okay. I heard Miranda's frantic voice saying I was having a panic attack. I couldn't focus on any of them. The words were drowning me. Suffocating me. I needed air.

"Move," Dank's voice broke into my fog and I managed to take a much-needed deep breath, coughing as air entered my lungs. "I've got you, Pagan. It's okay. I'm sorry," he murmured other things that I didn't understand, but they soothed me. My heart slowed down and the pounding subsided to a small ache. Dank was holding me and rocking me in his arms. His hand was caressing my head with gentle strokes. I was suddenly tired.

"She okay?" Gee asked from somewhere nearby.

"Yeah, she's breathing easy now," Dank replied.

"What the heck happened? She was fine one minute and the next minute she was in a full-blown panic attack. I know what it was because

I had several after my boyfriend died. I could see it all over her face. She couldn't breathe; she couldn't see." Miranda sounded upset.

I lifted my head from Dank's chest and looked up to see that Dank was sitting on the floor with his back against the wall and I was in his lap. Miranda knelt beside us wringing her hands frantically.

"I'm good. I don't know what happened. Something just snapped," I tried to explain. I decided against telling them that the words of his song had sent me spiraling out of control.

"It's the move. You've not gotten enough sleep. You're adjusting. I'm forcing you to go out places at night and then unloading all my screwed up emotions on you. I've cried on your shoulder and you've been the one to make me feel better. It's my fault. I need to stop being a big baby." I held up my hand to stop Miranda from her sudden need to take all the blame for this.

"I'm fine. Nothing is your fault. I don't know what triggered it, but I'm good now." I felt like an idiot curled up like a baby in Dank's arms. It was a miracle this guy hadn't sent me packing yet. I started to stand up and let him get back to the band. It sounded as if the other members were carrying on without him. He jumped up quickly and hovered beside me as if I was going to crumple to the ground.

"You're supposed to be out there," I told him nodding toward the stage.

"I can quit for the night. Do you want me to drive you back to your dorm?" His worried tone made this even more humiliating. I was the crazy, mentally unstable girl.

"No. Really. I am fine, but I do think I'm gonna go if Miranda is okay with that," I glanced over at her and she nodded in agreement.

"I can take you. She can stay and listen to the rest of the set," he said studying my face as if he was waiting on some answer to appear.

"I got this, Dank. Go do your thing. You have a long night ahead of you," Gee piped up and Dank shot her a warning glare. It was something I was used to seeing him direct her way. He did it a lot.

"I'm fine. You go sing," I assured him again and pushed him gently toward the stage entrance.

Dank's frown deepened and he started to shake his head no. Gee stepped forward and grabbed him by the arm and whispered something angrily in his ear. His defeated sigh bothered me, but when she was done, he nodded and looked back at me. "Okay. If you're sure you'll be okay. Just say the word and I'll take you back to the dorm."

"Positive," I replied.

Dank nodded and turned around and jogged back onto the stage. The crowd in the club erupted in cheers and chanted his name.

"Alright, Peggy Ann, let's get you out of here before he sings again. Apparently, it's your kryptonite."

Chapter Twelve

Dank

It was still early and students weren't littering the campus yet. I'd worked hard all night trying to keep the memory of Pagan's mental breakdown out of my head. She'd been about to remember. I reached up and touched the Celtic knot just under my shirt. This had triggered a memory. The song I wrote for her had sent her to her knees. The memories were there, trying to break free. But as much as I wanted her to remember, I knew the human mind was a fragile thing. Gee had reminded me last night that I could do damage to Pagan in my haste for her to get her memory back.

"Dankmar," Jaslyn, a transporter who also worked as a messenger, stepped out of the morning fog, and unlike Gee, looked every bit as unearthly as one would expect.

"Yes," I replied hesitantly. The last time she'd shown up to tell me something, it hadn't been pleasant.

"The Deity is not pleased. You are pushing the girl too hard. She hasn't even reconnected emotionally with her soul's mate. Her memory will not be restored until a fair decision can be made."

Why were they doing this? If she wasn't connecting with him, didn't that mean her heart was already claimed—memory or not? There was a reason she was unable to feel something for the soul who was created for her. "I'm not pushing. I'm waiting. But the soul they are expecting to mean something to her doesn't stand a chance. He isn't ready for any type of relationship either."

Jaslyn gave me a sad smile. "I am to tell you to be ready. It is coming. The souls will connect and when they do, you must stand back and let them. Death must not interfere. Your job is not to protect this girl. If she loves you, then she will come to you. Death can not go to her."

"They want me to back away?" I asked incredulously. That wasn't going to happen. If I had any chance at winning this, then I had to show her what she meant to me. Her heart knew it. Her mind just couldn't remember it.

"You are to be prepared for the souls to connect. It is what is meant to be. You are not her destiny. However, if at the time her soul has found its mate and her heart still wants you, then it will be her choice. Her memories will be restored. If she chooses her mate, then those memories will be lost forever."

I didn't reply. There was nothing left to say. I held the power to take life from a body, but that is where it ended. I could not control this. Fate wasn't mine to mold. Jaslyn faded away, leaving me with the message and warning. This wasn't going to happen as easily as I'd thought. The Deity knew the future. They knew what was coming next. Preparing myself for the rage that would consume me was the least of my worries.

Pagan

The banging on our door at eight in the morning was unwelcome. It was a Saturday and I wanted to sleep until late. Miranda groaned and grabbed her pillow to cover her head and ears.

"Who the hell is that?" she grumbled as I tried to shake the sleep from my fuzzy brain.

"I dunno, but they aren't going to live long," I replied, throwing the covers back and getting out of bed. I glanced down and realized I'd slept in sweats and a tank top. I was covered up enough. But then it was only eight, so the person beating down our door had to be a female. So being properly covered up didn't really matter.

I jerked the door open and the angry words I'd been about to say fell flat as I looked into the eyes of a very upset and determined Nathan.

"I tried to stop him," Jay said from behind him. I shifted my gaze off Nathan to Jay, then looked down the empty hall. How had they not woken up everyone with that banging?

"What is this?" I asked confused.

Nathan moved me out of the way with little force since I wasn't expecting it, and barged into the room. "She won't answer my calls and you won't allow me in the building when you're awake. So, I had Jay bribe a chick and get us inside while you weren't awake to stop me."

Miranda sat up in bed and the covers fell to her waist revealing the thin white camisole she'd slept in. I thought about telling her to cover up, but the shocked look on her face stopped me. It wasn't like they could actually see through it all the way.

"Nathan?" she croaked in a sleepy voice.

He went over and knelt down beside her bed, then pulled the blanket up to cover up her boobs. I had to give him points for that. "I need you to listen to me. I can't defend myself if you won't give me a chance."

I wasn't sure if Jay and I should step out of the room or if Miranda would want me there. So, I just stayed put by the door.

"It doesn't matter, I'm over it." That didn't even begin to sound convincing.

A doorknob across the hall started to turn and I grabbed Jay's arm and pulled him inside and closed the door quickly before we got caught with boys in our room. I wanted Nathan to get to say what he came here to say.

Both Nathan and Miranda looked back at us now standing in the room in front of the door. I shrugged, "The girls across the room are waking up," I explained.

Nathan nodded his head toward the bathroom, "Can y'all go in there and give us a little privacy?

"Sure," I replied, grabbing Jay's hand and tugging him along behind me. I wanted this matter settled and Miranda wasn't going to be easy to convince. We'd spent two full days eating ice cream and watching Damon to get her over this guy.

Once we were safely tucked away in the bathroom, I let go of Jay's hand and put some distance between us. In fact, this mess was his fault.

"What happened with them?" Jay asked as I pressed my back up against the door to Gee's room.

"You don't know?" I asked. Was he really *that* busy with his female friends that he hadn't even asked Nathan what had happened?

"Nathan doesn't really know either. From what you told him at the door the night he tried to get in, Victoria had shown up and shared his sexual habits with Miranda and she wasn't interested in being a part of that."

I hadn't been very clear, but I'd thought he would have figured it out if he was in fact screwing that girl on a regular basis. "Victoria showed up to warn me off you. Miranda was being defensive and trying to stand between the two of us. Then Victoria informed Miranda that Nathan was screwing some girl named Siera on a regular basis. She was his, and I quote, 'fuck buddy' and that Miranda needed to step back."

Jay's eyes went wide and he shook his head, "That shit ain't true. Nathan and Siera had a very short fling about two months ago. It was just sex. He didn't even like her very much. I think they may have had sex a few times since then, but only because he drank too much at a frat house party and she threw herself at him."

I nodded, "I kinda figured that. Hopefully that is all getting cleared up in there."

Jay took a step toward me, "What about you? What did Victoria say to you?"

"Oh, that you and her did it like rabbits and I needed to forget about you. You weren't interested in me. I was just a flavor of the week."

Nathan scowled and slammed his palm down on the counter. "I'm so fucking sick of her shit. I've told her no. I've pushed her away, but she is still convinced I want her."

"Are you trying to tell me y'all didn't do it like they do it on the Discovery Channel?" I asked in an amused tone.

Nathan frowned, "Sure, we've had sex a few times. She is one of the easier lays on campus. But I don't have any feelings for her. She was just handy. Now she's got it in her head that I want something more."

Nice. He was all about respecting the females these days. "Hmmm, it seems to me that maybe you should be more careful where you stick it."

Nathan sighed and leaned a hip against the sink. "This has ruined any small chance I might have had to get another date with you, hasn't it?"

I nodded, "Yep, pretty much. Although, if it makes you feel better, I was against the dating-you thing after you asked someone else out on our last date."

Nathan ran both hands through his hair and cursed under his breath. "I wasn't expecting you to walk back into my life, Pagan. I thought about you all the time, but I had been telling myself for over a year that you were gone. I'd never see you again. I didn't get serious with anyone because I always compared them to you. No one ever measures up. Yes, I've screwed around and dated a lot of girls, but it was my way of coping. If I'd known you'd be walking back into my life again, I'd have done things so very differently."

Well, that was nice. Didn't change how I felt, but it was still nice to hear.

The door opened and Miranda stuck her head in, "Could y'all maybe leave?"

"Uh, yeah, but could I have clothes first?" I asked, studying her very pleased expression.

"Yeah, hold on. Don't come out, though," she said slamming the door in our faces.

"I'm thinking my man might have smoothed things over," Jay said with a small laugh.

"Yeah, I'm thinking you're right."

The door inched open and a pair of cut-off blue denim shorts and a Rolling Stones tee shirt that was entirely too tight—which Miranda knew very well—was shoved through the door before it closed again. The lock clicked and I looked over at Jay.

"You're gonna have to leave through Gee's door before I get dressed."

Jay grinned, "I promise to close my eyes."

"Not in a million years," I assured him and bent over to pick up my clothes.

"Come on, Pagan, I promise I won't look."

He had to be kidding me. When had I ever been willing to change in front of him?

I knocked on Gee's door and when I got no reply, I opened it. Peeking inside, I found it empty. Good. At least she didn't have to see me sneaking out of the bathroom with Jay. "Coast is clear. Now, go away."

Jay stuck out his bottom lip in a pout and I shoved him out the door and locked myself inside.

CHAPTER THIRTEEN

Dank

The soul that threatened my success in winning Pagan back came walking out of her dorm while I was waiting for her to come outside. I swung my leg over my Harley and stood up. What the hell was he doing in her dorm?

"Gee," I said quietly knowing that she would hear me no matter where she was. There had better be a really good reason for the silly smile on his face. He glanced up at the window to Pagan's room. I fisted both hands and stalked toward him. I wasn't sure what I was going to say or do, but I had to know why he'd been in her room.

"Whoa, slow down, Cowboy; where you going?" Gee grabbed my arm as she appeared at my side.

"To kick his sorry ass," I replied and jerked my arm from her grasp.

"No. You are not. This is supposed to happen. Remember? She is going to reconnect with her soul mate. Their souls have to connect, Dank. Chill the fuck down!"

I knew this. I hated it, but I knew it. "Why is he coming out of her dorm so damned early in the morning and where were you, anyway?"

Gee smirked, "I'm sure it wasn't anything like what you are thinking. Pagan isn't even into him yet. And as for where I was—let's just say your drummer is a happy boy this morning."

"Not Loose again. You can't get attached, Gee," I warned her. My thoughts were disrupted when the door to her building opened and Pagan stepped outside. My heart slammed against my chest at the site of her. She was in a pair of shorts that were entirely too short for her to wear in public, and her shirt left nothing to the imagination. I saw her frown and followed her gaze to the boy waiting for her. Screw the rules. I wasn't standing here and letting her go anywhere with him, especially dressed like that.

"Dank, don't," Gee called out from behind me, but I ignored her and kept walking. I didn't need a lecture from her when she had been screwing the drummer, again.

Pagan's gaze swung around and her eyes met mine. A small smile touched her lips and I wanted to pound my chest in jubilation. She was happy to see me. She hadn't smiled at him. She'd smiled at me.

"Dank?" The surprise in her voice was accompanied by a pleased gleam in her eyes.

"Good morning," I replied trying to think of a way I could get her to go inside and change without sounding like a jerk.

"What are you doing here?"

Waiting to see you.

Her eyes flew open wide and I realized I'd unintentionally talked to her soul again. I had to stop doing that. "I was up early and thought I'd stop by and see if you wanted to have breakfast with me."

Her smile faltered as her brain worked through the fact she'd heard me speak in her head.

"Pagan? You coming?" Jay asked keeping his distance from us. I made him nervous; I could feel his fear.

Pagan frowned and looked over at him, "Coming where?"

That's my girl. Shoot him down.

"I thought we would go get a coffee and talk while they, you know—" he pointed toward her room.

Pagan looked back at me and I seriously considered begging. She pressed her lips together then turned her eyes back toward Jay. "Uh, actu ally, no. I thought you were leaving. I'm sure Nathan will find a way back. Miranda has a car."

She was choosing me. The urge to reach out and pull her close to me possessively was overwhelming, but I kept myself in check.

"You going with him?" Jay asked harshly. I cut my eyes in his direction and he stiffened. Yeah, he better get the warning.

"Yes, Jay, I am. Not that it is any of your business."

I was kissing her as soon as he left us the hell alone.

Jay opened his mouth and I pulled back my lips in a snarl. He stopped. Smart boy.

Shaking his head, he turned and walked off.

I reached down and threaded my fingers through hers. "Let's go eat."

She smiled down at our hands, then looked up at me," Okay. Where to?"

I pulled her closer to me, "Anywhere you want."

She looked around me and saw my Harley parked across the street. "Are we taking that?" she asked.

"If that's okay. I can promise you that you will be completely safe."

She bit down on her bottom lip several times as she contemplated it. Finally, she nodded. "Okay, yeah. Let's take it."

I'd brought a helmet with me just in case she agreed to ride with me. Pulling it out of the back compartment, I put it on her head and fastened it. She was adorable. I really should have gotten one of these sooner. She'd have been hot riding to school with me every morning on the back of a Harley.

"How do I look?" she asked.

"Hot. Smoking hot."

A blush covered her cheeks and she ducked her head to hide it. I got on the bike and held my hand out to her. "Come here."

She slipped her hand in mine and I held her steady as she lifted her leg over the back and scooted in against my back. When she slid her arms around me and her hands grabbed tightly to the tee shirt covering my stomach, I closed my eyes and sighed. Yeah, this was good. Really good.

Pagan

Riding the back of a motorcycle pressed up tightly against Dank Walker was one of those experiences that all females should have before they die. Nothing compared to it. The dark exotic smell that was his alone invaded my senses. My fingers and palms kept grazing his abs and, oh my, were his abs nice. Unlike other abs I'd seen, his were really, really ripped. He had more than just a six-pack. I fought the need to slip my hands under his shirt just to see what the skin covering such a perfect stomach felt like.

Dank got off the bike and helped me get off. I was a little unsteady, but it worked out to my advantage because he took my waist and pulled me up against his chest. Now I knew what that chest felt like. And it was nice. So very nice.

"I liked that. A lot." He told me in a low sexy voice.

I swallowed hard and nodded. Might as well be honest. "Yeah, me too." I glanced down at his stomach. I really wanted to see it bare.

"What you looking at, Pagan?" The amused tone in his voice didn't mask the fact he was turned on.

I decided to be brave. "I was wondering what your stomach looks like. After our ride, I have a few ideas, but—" I trailed off.

Dank's hands squeezed my waist and he took a deep breath, "If you want me to take my shirt off, I'd be more than happy to oblige. However, can we do it when there are no people around us?"

I nodded and pressed my lips together to keep from laughing. I'd just asked a guy to take off his shirt. Had I ever done something like that before? It was liberating.

Dank took my hand and we walked into a cute little café engulfed in delicious aromas. It was a seat-yourself kind of place, so Dank led us to a far corner table for two. He pulled out my chair for me; I was positive no one had ever done that before.

Once he was seated, he leaned forward and his blue eyes were almost close to the glowing look they often got. "I don't know how I'm going to eat now. All I can think about is the fact you want my shirt off."

Giggling, I covered my mouth and looked around. The place was busy, but not too crowded. We had a small amount of privacy where we were sitting. "Sorry. I shouldn't have said that."

Dank's eyes flared and he reached over and grabbed my hand, "No. If you want something, ask me. Anything."

Um. Okay. His reaction was, uh, a little intense. But then I was getting used to Dank's intensity. He definitely seemed interested in me. There was no question about that. He liked me as much as I liked him.

"Can I get you something to drink?" A chipper voice asked and I jerked my hand back, startled by the interruption.

"Pagan?" Dank asked, looking at me instead of the waitress. I lifted my attention from him to the girl who wasn't looking at me at all. She was drinking in Dank. I couldn't blame her. Not one bit.

"Orange juice, please." She nodded and scribbled it down, then looked wistfully at Dank.

"Milk," he replied still watching me.

"Here are your menus. I'll be back in a few minutes to take your order," she told Dank, who ignored her.

"Thanks," I replied.

She left and I looked back at Dank. "You're making me nervous looking at me like that," I told him.

He frowned and leaned back in his seat. "I'm sorry."

Great. Now he looked worried. How did someone like him appear so hard and untouchable one minute, then sensitive and vulnerable the next? He was one big contradiction.

"Don't apologize. I haven't had a shower and I have no makeup on. I wasn't expecting to see you this morning when Miranda kicked me out of the room with nothing but these clothes to put on."

Dank smirked, "You look perfect. You always do." Then he paused and leaned forward again, "Why did Miranda kick you out?"

"Nathan came to apologize this morning. He woke us up banging on our door. Jay was with him. Anyway, I'm not sure yet what he said to make it better between them because she kicked us out. I'm pretty sure they were getting busy which was why she threw clothes at me and told me to go away."

"That explains this morning. I was worried I had some competition."

There was a competition? For me? Oh my.

"No, right now you're the only one I'm interested in spending more time with."

The pleased grin that lit up his face was worth putting myself out there.

Our drinks were placed in front of us and I realized I hadn't even looked at a menu. Dank explained to the waitress that we needed a few more minutes.

Chapter Fourteen

Pagan

I managed to wake up with my alarm clock this morning, so I had time to make a quick stop to the coffee shop. That meant I would be more awake during class. Miranda was still sleeping when I left. Her first class of the day wasn't until eleven, so this was her morning to sleep late. Unfortunately, I hadn't been blessed with one of those late starts on my schedule.

After spending Saturday morning with Dank, I'd gone to the library and found the other books I needed for my Literature class. Then I'd called it an early night. Miranda had gone out with Nathan and not returned until seven on Sunday morning. I'd once again been woken up entirely too early for a weekend. She'd insisted we spend the day shopping for new underwear and shoes.

I'd texted back and forth with Dank some and he'd called once, but I hadn't seen him. Not that he hadn't tried. Miranda had just consumed my entire day on Sunday. Then that night when she had gone out with Nathan again, Dank wasn't around. At least I got to bed early.

The line at the coffee shop was not moving very quickly. I glanced down at my phone to check the time—I had fifteen minutes before class. The walk from here was about five, so I knew I would be on time.

Finally, the blond guy in front of me moved. He was holding two cups of coffee and smiling at me. I returned the smile and waited for him to actually walk away so I could step up and order my morning caffeine, but the guy wasn't budging. He held out one of the coffees to me. What was he doing? Sharing? Um, no thanks. I was picky about my latte.

"Caramel latte with whipped cream. Just for you," the happy stranger said. How had he known what I was going to order? And why did he order it for me? Was he a stalker? Should I call the police?

"Next, please," the guy behind the counter said in an annoyed tone. We were holding up the line.

"Take it. The guy just made it. I can't drink two of them." The sincere kindness in his eyes sold me. Maybe he was just a lucky guesser. Or maybe I should really call the cops.

I took the cup from his hand and stepped out of the line. The girl behind me sighed loudly and mumbled, "Finally. Thank you."

I took a sip of the coffee and realized it really was exactly how I liked it. I should at least thank him and be polite. I'd think about the restraining order later. "Um, thanks for the coffee. Not sure how you knew what I wanted, but thanks. I'm gonna be late for class, so this helps out."

"Can I walk you?" he asked moving with me as I made my way to the door.

"Uh, yeah, I guess. Do you go here?" I asked as he fell in step beside me.

He chuckled softly and the hairs on my arms stood up. Not a good sign. I stopped drinking my coffee. Something was off here.

"I'm just a local," was his reply. A local serial killer whose clutches I may have just walked into. "I have to admit I took an educated guess with your coffee and got lucky. I was trying to impress you with my chivalry. It looks like I've scared you instead. I didn't mean to."

He was observant. I'd give him that. Nodding, I still didn't take another drink of the latte. This entire situation was beginning to annoy me. I didn't have a coffee I could safely drink and I was going to be late for class if this guy didn't leave me alone.

"I was curious. Do you have a boyfriend?" Well, he was straightforward at least. I could lie and send him packing or I could answer honestly and run toward my building.

"Um, not that it is your business, but no." Now, should I run?

"So, you and Dankmar, I mean Dank Walker, aren't a thing?" Wait… What? How did he know about Dank? Was he a fan? Maybe this was one of Dank's stalkers.

"Uh, no. I just met Dank Walker," I replied stepping up my pace. The guy paused and I thought I was going to get away from him until I heard him jogging up beside me.

"You didn't know him before college? Like in high school?" What was the deal with this guy's questions? Oh. Questions…he had to be one of those gossip magazine reporters. That had to be it. I didn't realize Cold Soul was that big yet. I was being harassed by the paparazzi.

"Listen, I just met the guy. I know nothing about him. Leave me alone," I snapped and shoved my coffee back at him before turning and breaking into a run to get across the street before the light turned. I'd have to tell Dank about this. Or Dankmar…was that his real name?

"Whoa, Peggy Ann. Who ya running from?" Gee asked stepping in front of me as I reached the Science building.

"Some whacko nosey guy. I'm thinking he was a gossip reporter. He was asking me about my relationship with Dank. Or Dankmar, as he called him."

Gee's amused look vanished and she turned her head back toward the street I'd just crossed. A snarl appeared on her face. I glanced back and sure enough, the guy was still standing there watching us, both hands holding a coffee cup each.

"You know him? Because he seriously creeped me out."

Gee shook her head, "Voodoo boy doesn't know when to quit."

"Voodoo boy?" I asked confused.

Gee turned her gaze back to me, "Nothing. Water under the bridge and shit. Come on, we actually have a class together. This will entertain me. Oh, and here, take this! It's from lover boy." She shoved a backpack into my arms.

"What's this?" I asked confused.

"You needed a laptop and Dank delivered. Come on," Gee said and spun around in her black leather combat boots and stalked toward the building. I had to hurry to keep up.

I'd forgotten he'd mentioned letting me use his other laptop. This would make my week so much easier. Mom still hadn't gotten enough money to order one for me. I would be sure to thank him properly as soon as I saw him.

I'd been hoping to see Dank this morning, but there was no way we had more than two classes together. At least, I had Gee in this one. Well…maybe that wasn't such a good thing. She might end up being more distracting than anything.

* * * *

Gee had actually flirted with the professor. Heavily. As in made him blush bright red several times. The man stammered all over himself through most of the class. It was more entertaining than anything. I hadn't learned one thing. At least, he had given us some references and a website with this week's assignments.

"I can't believe you," I said, laughing as we walked to the dorm. I had three hours before Calculus with Dank.

Gee shrugged, "What? He was a cutie. The quiet nerdy kind. I like to fuck with their heads. Besides, that shit is boring in there. I got better things to do."

"If you want to pass this class, then you had better pay more attention to what he is saying than how to make him blush." Although, it was funny to watch.

"Subject change. The guy this morning. Stay away from him if you see him again."

Did she know him? Her comment about 'Voodoo boy' had bothered me, but Gee was weird and often said off-the-wall things. I'd blown it off. Now, I was becoming concerned. "Is he dangerous?" I asked glancing back to see if we were being followed. Maybe that call to the cops wasn't such a bad idea.

"He won't hurt you. Trust me. Just avoid him. He'll disappear soon enough."

Must be paparazzi like I'd assumed. Cold Soul's lead singer couldn't hold their interest too long. Not when they had movie stars behaving badly to chase down.

When we turned the corner and the front of our dorm came into view, I saw Dank leaning against his motorcycle with his arms crossed over his chest talking to a couple of girls. He looked very disinterested and his eyes immediately found mine. He didn't say anything to them as he straightened up and walked away from them and toward me. That was the way I wanted a guy I was considering dating to act when he was being flirted with by other girls. I couldn't keep the silly smile off my face.

"Looks like Romeo was waiting for your return."

Dank

If my time with Pagan was limited before her soul began connecting to Jay's, then I was going to make damn sure that she couldn't get me out of her head. I'd spent all morning planning our evening. Now, I just had to get her to agree.

Gee muttered, "Pagan got some Bourbon Street coffee this morning," as she walked past me on her way into the dorm.

I didn't need an explanation. I had warned Leif, but now I was ready to act on my warning. She didn't remember him. His time with her was over. Him staying around was only going to confuse her.

"Hey," Pagan said in way of greeting. She had stopped in front of me. She didn't look upset or scared. Whatever Leif said to her hadn't made an impact. Ghede really needed to find his kid a hobby. Pagan was no longer available for his entertainment.

"Good morning. How was class?"

She shrugged, then an amused smile broke out on her face, "Gee made the professor a nervous blubbering wreck with her flirting."

Leave it to Gee to cause a stir wherever she went. "Is that so? I take it you enjoyed the show."

Pagan let out a small laugh, "Yes, I did. I probably shouldn't have, but it was too funny to ignore. But it was so much easier taking notes on the laptop you sent me. Thank you so much. I promise to take good care of it."

"Dank Walker! Oh, wow, I saw you last week at Club Butter. You were amazing," a girl stepped in front of Pagan and laid her hand on my chest as she began to prattle off some more. I reached for her wrist and removed her hand from my body, then reached around her and grabbed Pagan's hand and pulled her toward me.

"Thanks, I'm glad you enjoyed the show. If you'll excuse us, we were having a private conversation," I informed her. She shifted her eyes from me to Pagan and an unimpressed smirk distorted her face. I slipped my hand around Pagan's waist and pulled her closer to my side. She came willingly.

"Oh, well, when you want a little more excitement, I can be found right back here," she pointed at the dorm. Pagan had to live in the same building with her. I needed to make Gee aware that this one could be vindictive.

"I'm sure that will never be the case," I replied.

The girl spun around and stalked off angrily. She wasn't used to being turned down.

"What is it with her? She goes after every guy I date."

Pagan's response caused me to tense up. What other guys had she been dating? I wasn't aware she'd been out with anyone other than Jay. Had Gee been keeping something from me?

"Really?" I managed to ask in a normal voice, tamping down the anger and jealousy rolling through me. Pagan couldn't see that.

"Yeah, really. But at least you didn't set up a date with her right in front of me. Jay made plans with her while on a date with me. I didn't care exactly, but it was a little embarrassing. Did nothing for my ego."

He was an ass. How could he be her soul's mate? They didn't match up. He was far from worthy. "The guy is an idiot. There is no comparison between the two of you. She can't compete with you."

Pagan inhaled sharply, then turned her face up to look at me, "Okay, yeah, you're really good at this, Dank Walker. Really good."

"I'm glad you like your laptop. Feel free to use the bag it came in to carry your other books. Will you ride with me to our next class?" I asked pulling out her helmet.

The corner of her mouth turned up and she reached for the helmet. "Thank you. I'll do that and, yeah, I think I will take a lift."

Chapter Fifteen

Pagan

I had a date with Dank. A real date, not an impromptu breakfast, but a real date. Just us. I was equally excited as I was nervous. And I wasn't sure what to wear. This must have been the way Miranda felt when she was getting ready to go out with Nathan.

"You can pull off the boy shorts and bra well, but I'm thinking clothing may be required for where you're going tonight," Gee said as she walked into the room through our adjoining bathroom without knocking.

"Funny," I replied frowning at her. "I can't decide what to wear. He said I could dress however I wanted to, but that isn't very helpful."

"I'm thinking he didn't mean clothing was optional," Gee drawled as she plopped down on my bed.

"You think? Thanks for clueing me in. I was thinking I might just parade around in my undies all night."

Gee laughed, "On second thought, he'd probably like that. I still vote for clothes though."

"Should I wear casual or dressy? Which would he prefer?" I asked Gee as I scanned my limited wardrobe.

"You want my honest opinion?"

I glanced back at her over my shoulder, "Yes. I do. You know him better than I do."

Gee nodded in agreement. "Okay, wear that pink dress with those pink heels. He'll be a puddle at your feet."

The pink dress? Really? I wasn't even sure why I owned that dress. I had never worn it before. I reached for the hanger it was on and pulled it out. It was sexy in an innocent kind of way. Might have been a little dressy, but then he hadn't said not to be dressy. I remembered how he'd picked up those heels and held them like they were precious. Maybe he had a thing for pink heels.

"You wear that and he won't be able to concentrate. I can promise you that."

Gee knew him well. I'd go with her opinion. "Okay. If you say so."

Two hours later, I was shaved, plucked, dressed and ready, when someone knocked on my door. Who was that? I needed to go meet Dank in the great hall in five minutes. Miranda was still out with Nathan. They'd had a lunch date that was still going strong according to her many text messages. Gee had bailed on me after I started painting my toenails. She had lived through all the primping she could handle.

I opened the door to find Dank standing there in a pair of khaki slacks, a black dress shirt that was left open at the collar and, of course, his boots, holding a dozen red roses. He looked mouthwatering. His surprised expression as he took in what I was wearing didn't go unnoticed. What was he surprised about? That I could clean up nicely?

"Pagan, you, uh, wow, I…I really like you in pink."

I really liked this side of him. The not so cool and confident side. The one that seemed emotionally exposed. I smiled and pointed to the roses, "Are those for me?"

He glanced down at the forgotten flowers in his hand and chuckled, "Yeah, they are." He held them out for me to take and I realized this was a first. No guy had ever brought me roses before.

"Thank you," I replied stepping back to let him in. If he'd been spotted in the hall, someone would have said something by now. I wanted to put my first ever roses in water before we left and leaving him in the hall was a bad idea. However, I didn't have a vase in here. I scanned the room for something to put my roses in.

"What about this?" Dank asked walking over to my desk and picking up my empty pencil holder that Miranda had insisted we buy to match our other cute desk items. It was perfect.

"Yes! It finally comes in useful," I took the pencil holder and went to the bathroom to clean it out and fill it with water. When I walked back into the room, Dank was standing in front of my bulletin board looking at the pictures I'd pinned up there from high school. Several had Wyatt in them. A few had my mother, but most were just Miranda and me. I didn't have that many pictures of my years in high school. Especially my senior year. There was nothing. Sometimes, I couldn't even remember things like my prom or who was in my class. Everything seemed blurry. My mom said it was the trauma of losing Wyatt that messed with my head. Miranda felt the same way, so that made sense. She'd lost her boyfriend, but we'd both lost one of our best friends.

"That's Wyatt," I explained as I walked up to stand beside him. "He was Miranda's boyfriend and a close friend of mine. He died last year."

Dank nodded his head. There was a sadness there, almost like he understood that kind of pain. Had he lost someone too? "I'm sure that was tough."

Yeah it was awful. "I hate death. It's a tragic thing that comes for us all. For some sooner than others."

Dank's shoulders tensed and he shifted away from me. What had I said? This was not what I wanted to be talking about tonight. Death was so morbid and sad. "I'm sorry. I shouldn't have even brought up such a sad topic."

I watched as Dank stared out the window instead of looking at me. He was dealing with something. I just wished I knew what. After what felt like several minutes, but was probably only seconds in reality, he turned his attention toward me. "Death can't help what fate decides."

That was much deeper than anything I'd expected to come out of his mouth. He was right, so I nodded, "That's true. I guess we can't blame death for the tragedy. Fate isn't something anyone can control."

Dank let out a heavy sigh. The guy must have had to deal with death one too many times in his life. Way to go, Pagan. Bring up something upsetting and screw up the mood. "Are you ready?" he asked finally breaking the uncomfortable silence.

"Yes."

Dank motioned for me to lead the way and he opened the door for me. I made sure no one was around before he followed me out. The tension in the air around us was thick. I knew it was my fault, even though I didn't know what I'd said exactly to make him so uncomfortable. I could either force him to explain what I'd said wrong or let this go for fear of ruining our evening. Perhaps he would open up to me willingly another time. I didn't get the vibe from him that this was something he wanted to talk about.

When we stepped out into the parking lot, I was about to offer Miranda's car for us when I noticed a limo waiting at the curb. Dank flashed me a crooked smile, "I couldn't make you ride on the back of a motorcycle in a dress and heels."

How had he known I was wearing a dress and heels?

"Gee," he replied without me asking him.

"Ah, that makes sense, but Miranda had told me we could use her car. I knew your motorcycle and my dress wouldn't make a good combination."

"This will be more fun," he winked, opened the door and assisted me inside. The driver didn't get out. I thought that was odd, but I didn't question it.

Dank

Having Pagan sitting so close to me and wearing that little pink dress I loved that showed off her legs eased the pain in my chest caused by her earlier words about hating death. She hadn't known what she was saying; in her mind death was an event, not a being. Most humans saw it that way. My job brought neither fame nor popularity. I took souls. The things humans cherished the most. Pagan had lost Wyatt. She hated death because of that loss, despite of the fact that it wasn't Death's fault he was gone.

"So, can you tell me where we are going now?" she asked. I could see the worried look in her eyes. I needed to snap out of this. She was feeling my mood and I didn't want tonight to be screwed up because of this. She hadn't meant it when she'd said she hated death. It hadn't meant she hated me. But not being able to hear her tell me she loved me was getting to me. Not being able to see that love and devotion in her eyes made every day look bleak.

"We'll be there soon. Are you always this impatient?" I smiled at her so she knew I was teasing and her shoulders relaxed. I had upset her with my earlier reaction.

"Yes, as a matter of fact, I am," she replied.

"I may have the driver ride around a little longer just for fun."

Pagan shoved me with her shoulder, "Don't underestimate me. I can take you down."

And I would gladly let her.

"You think so? I think watching you try would be the highlight of my year."

Pagan raised both her eyebrows and with a challenging look, she bent over to take off her heels. What the heck? She placed them both on the seat across from us and then turned her attention to me. "You sure about this because my size can be deceiving?"

"If you mean to tell me that you're about to jump on any part of my body, then please, Pagan, by all means, *bring it on.*"

Her face instantly turned bright red. Damn. She was going to back out.

"Uh," she said staring at me like she wasn't sure what her next move was going to be.

"You're about to show me how easily you can take me down. Don't go getting shy now after you got my hopes up."

Pagan ducked her head and let out a small laugh. I took advantage of the situation, moved quickly and had her lying back on the seat while I held myself over her before she knew what was happening.

"Gotcha. Now, what you gonna do?" I asked as her startled look turned into a calculating gleam. She leaned up and covered my lips with hers before I knew what she was doing. Her small, even, white teeth nibbled on my bottom lip and then her tongue took a small swipe before easing into my very eager mouth. Her hands were on my chest and moving downward, making all normal thought flee. I could only focus on one thing: Pagan and how she felt, tasted, and the small little pleased sounds coming from her throat.

Her hands shoved me back and her legs wrapped around my waist. I moved back pulling her with me and she maneuvered her body until she on top of me straddling my lap. I buried my hands in her hair as she squeezed the sides of my waist, then slowly pulled back. The triumphant grin on her face was adorable.

"Who's on top now? Don't ever underestimate me," she said in a husky voice.

If I hadn't already been completely owned by this female, I would have been now. This was my Pagan.

CHAPTER SIXTEEN

Pagan

The first thing I saw through the tinted windows of the limo was twinkling white lights. There were thousands of them. I scooted over to look closer and see where exactly the driver had taken us. I'd just spent more than ten minutes in Dank's lap, kissing and being kissed senseless.

The large area looked like a field with a gazebo covered in white lights sitting in the middle of it. Strands of lights were strung from the gazebo to the trees surrounding it, stretching like a canopy of lights around it. What was this place?

The limo came to a stop and I looked back at Dank who was watching me instead of looking out the window. "Where are we?" I asked.

Dank smirked that sexy way of his and the driver opened my door. I slid out and Dank followed me. He thanked the tall, dark man who then got back into the car and drove away.

I looked around at this secluded site that Dank had obviously taken great pains to make it appear so stunning.

"It's not the Garden of the Hesperides, but then who wants to eat golden apples and dodge a dragon. This garden is a much better option."

Had the rocker just compared this place to Hera's garden? Impressive. But then again, he frequently managed to surprise me.

"It's gorgeous. How did you do all this?" I asked as he took my elbow and led me toward the gazebo.

"I have my ways."

He was always so secretive. I shouldn't have really expected him to actually tell me how he'd managed to get a large elaborate gazebo into the middle of a deserted field and then cover the place in lights.

The three steps on the gazebo were lined with white lights. A small round table sat in the center of the covered area, a silver tablecloth draping it and with two chairs placed around it. A bouquet of some kind of exotic flowers I'd never seen before sat in the middle of the table. Even the glass vase had lights inside it. He had really put a lot of work into this. I was suddenly very thankful that I hadn't worn jeans.

"What are you thinking?" he asked close to my ear. I shivered from the warmth of his breath against my skin.

"I'm thinking you either must really want to impress me or this is something you've invested in to bring all your first dates to." I was teasing, of course, and I smiled at him as I said it so he'd know I wasn't being serious.

"Never realized how sexy a smart mouth could be," he replied.

Soft music began playing from speakers hidden in the corners of the gazebo. Dank held out his hand, "Dance with me?"

I slid my hand into his and he pulled me against his chest. This was different from our first dance at the club. It was sweeter, more intimate. It felt like it was less about our attraction and more about the connection between us.

"Pagan?" Dank asked softly against my ear.

"Yes," I replied resting my chin on his shoulder thanks to my height in heels.

"Will you promise me something?"

He sounded vulnerable. I thought about it a minute, then nodded. "Yes."

He let out another heavy sigh. Something was bothering him tonight. "One day you'll need to remember this. Remember how this felt. I need you to tuck this memory close inside and hold onto it."

That was by far the oddest thing anyone had ever said or asked of me. He almost sounded like he was dying. "Um, okay," I replied hesitantly.

He let out a soft chuckle, "I'm sorry. Sometimes I can get a little too intense."

No kidding. He took my hand and lifted it in the air, twirling me around. I decided I'd forget how strange his ominous request felt for now and enjoy the most romantic date I'd ever been on.

After the song ended, Dank walked over to the table and pulled out a chair for me. "I know it looks like we're out here all alone, but I don't intend to starve you."

I looked around and sure enough, a man in a tuxedo came walking out of the woods carrying a silver tray and two glass bottles of Coke.

Smiling back at Dank, I said, "I can't believe you set all this up."

He winked at me. "I wanted to make a good impression since this is our first official date."

"Well, you blew any other first dates I've ever had out of the water already, so sit back and relax."

Dank laughed as the waiter placed the Cokes in front of us and opened them. He lifted the lid on the silver tray and then took two glasses of ice from it and put them beside our bottles.

"I don't know how you could even think I'd ever be able to forget this," I said in awe as the server set chocolate-covered strawberries in front of us.

"Good. That's the idea," he replied.

* * * *

It had almost been a whole day since I'd seen or heard from Dank. He had brought me home after our date last night and I'd half expected him to be waiting on me outside the dorm this morning when I walked out. Then I'd been expecting him to be waiting on me outside the building of our first class. But he hadn't shown up for Literature again. After lunch, when he still hadn't called or shown up, I began to wonder if I'd done something wrong last night. Since the first day we'd met, he had managed to show up at least two times a day. I'd thought after the evening we'd had, he would be around even more. I had looked forward to seeing him. I'd almost texted him several times, but I'd refrained. He had my number.

Now that the sun was setting and he hadn't even bothered to text, I decided last night might have meant more to me than it had to him. Maybe that really was a setup for all his first dates. Maybe it hadn't meant anything more to him.

I stacked up my books and stuck them into my book bag. I'd spent the last two hours in the library studying. Miranda was getting ready for another date with Nathan and she was too chatty to allow me to get anything done. But being on my own hadn't been much better. My thoughts had kept going back to last night, wondering what I could have done wrong.

The night breeze was abnormally cool tonight. I pulled my books higher on my shoulder and made my way toward the dorm. It was almost a mile, but I figured the walk was good exercise. I didn't like trying to park Miranda's SUV. I could see myself scratching it.

"Dank, stop," a giggling female voice came from the darkness. My blood froze. Stopping in my tracks, I waited to listen for more. Surely, I'd heard that wrong.

"I want a taste," a familiar deep voice replied. My stomach felt sick.

"I can't get naked out here. Someone might come by," the girl whispered and then let out a small moan.

"Open your legs," he replied.

I wanted to move my legs. I wanted to move away from the voices. But I couldn't. My legs weren't cooperating.

"Right here?" the girl asked breathlessly.

"Yeah," he said, a small groan coming from him. I was going to be sick.

"Ah, Dank, mmmmm, that feels so good."

I took off running. I didn't look back. My heart felt as if Dank Walker had just broken it.

Dank

I'd worked all day to make up for my late night with Pagan. Tonight, however, I intended to spend it with her again. I walked into the empty park just outside of Pagan's dorm before appearing. Leif sat on the bench facing the dorm with one leg crossed over his knee and his arms folded across his chest. What was he still doing here? She didn't know him nor did she want to. Now that her soul was free of his claim, she couldn't even remember him from one week to the next. A week from now, she'd forget all about the strange guy who'd ordered her coffee correctly and questioned her. She had a soul. He didn't. There could never be a lasting connection. A spirit born of Voodoo could never connect with a soul born of the Creator. It was that simple. He knew it too.

"Why are you here?" I didn't bother to announce my arrival.

"Because I owed you one," was his only reply.

What the hell did that mean? I glared down at him, "Explain that."

Leif shrugged. "Not much to explain, Dankmar. You took Pagan from me. She'll never remember me. I lost all I'd ever known and loved. So, I thought you deserved the same thing in return."

He still made no sense. I knew Pagan was safe. He could no longer touch her soul. I held the life of her soul in my hands. "She never chose you. She chose me. You have no power here."

Leif stood up and took a step back away from me. Neither he nor his father liked to get too close to me. They knew their place in the scheme of things. My power was never-ending; theirs was conjured by the beliefs of humans. The weight of power lay heavily in my court.

"Let's just say, we're even now. If you're lucky, you'll figure it out, but the damage is done. Goodbye, Dankmar," Leif glanced at Pagan's dorm one more time before he vanished.

His solemn tone was the only thing that concerned me. He seemed worried about something. Unsure. He only had feelings for one person. No one else weighed on his conscience. *Pagan.*

I had to find her. Closing my eyes, I sensed her soul. It was hurting. My body echoed her pain. I didn't want her hurting. What had he done? She was in the dorm. I snapped my eyes open to find Gee standing in front of me.

"You're in a shitload of trouble. I can't figure it out exactly, but I know it's all kinds of fucked up." Gee shook her head and pointed back to the window of Pagan's room. "She thinks you were doing the wild thing behind the library with some chick. She is positive it was you. The girl called your name out and you talked back to her. It ain't pretty."

Fuck.

"It ain't like she is in love with you since she can't remember who the hell you are, but she obviously feels betrayed. She is spouting off about listening to her first instincts and how glad she is that she found this out sooner rather than later. That rockers are shitheads and that you are scum. Also that she hates she let you get so close. She feels like her heart is breaking. I think that about covers it."

I sank onto the bench and buried my head in my hands. How the hell was I going to fix this? I'd made progress. When Jay's soul started connecting with hers, I was going to have the upper hand. I was going to have found a way into her heart again. But now? She thought I had screwed some other girl? Outside? When?

"When did this happen?" I asked Gee.

"She came slamming into the room about fifteen minutes ago. Calling you very colorful names I didn't even know she was aware existed while tears ran down her face."

We're even now.

Leif's words replayed in my head. He'd been watching the window to her room. He had been acting as if something was bothering him. Pagan was upset. He knew why. He had done this. I'd taken Pagan from him and he'd returned the favor.

"Leif," I said as I looked back up at her window.

'What? You think that stupid Voodoo spawn did this?"

I nodded, "I know he did. He was paying me back."

"Fuck that. I'm gonna go beat his ass," Gee snarled.

"I need you up there with her, Gee. I need you to make sure she's okay. Watch out for her. I've got to find a way to fix this, but she isn't going to let me near her right now."

Gee sighed, "I want to go kick Voodoo ass. Not listen to a bitching female."

"Please, Gee."

"Fine. I'll go. But you need to think of something to tell her."

I nodded, "I know."

Gee left to do as I requested.

Chapter Seventeen

Pagan

Two days of dodging Dank and ignoring Gee every time she attempted to bring him up was beginning to wear on me. This was stupid. I'd been on *one* real date with Dank Walker. I'd kissed him a few times and I'd fallen under the sexy charisma he had going for him. Every girl falls for a boy in a band at some point. It happens. It's life. You learn from it and move on. I just wish I could do that. I wish I hadn't fallen for him so easily. The betrayal of it sliced through me every time I remembered their voices. But was that even really betrayal? We weren't a couple. We'd made no promises to each other. Dank could screw a girl outside of a building if he wanted to. I was just too stupid to know better than to think he felt more for me than he did. I had obviously been the only one with the deeper emotions.

I spent the weekend studying alone in my room. It was Monday morning and Dank would be in my next class. I'd smile and be polite and detached. No reason to act like anything happened. It wasn't like he had called all weekend or texted me. I was sure he knew about me hearing his sex party outside because Gee knew. Unfortunately, she'd been there right after I'd heard it, so she had seen my immediate reaction. I really, really hoped she hadn't shared that scene with Dank. I would have to pretend she hadn't if I was going to face him today.

I'd gotten a little wrapped up in the romance of it all and that was my first mistake.

Opening the door to Calculus, I realized that last week Dank had carried my books inside for me. He'd brought me to class on the back of his motorcycle. My life had been exciting for two weeks. It was time for me to focus on my studies. I didn't scan the room to see if Dank was already there. I found an empty seat and focused on getting in it instead of searching for him with my eyes all over the room. If he was sitting with this week's flavor, I might have difficulty paying close attention to the professor.

Dropping my books on my desk, I pulled out my pencils and a notebook. I'd returned his laptop to Gee and told her to make sure he got it back. I no longer needed it. That was of course untrue, but I had been pissed.

When a tingling sensation ran down my spine, I knew without even looking that the shadow that had fallen over my desk belonged to Dank. *Dangit.*

"Can I sit here?" His voice was husky and free of humor.

We had a room full of people and the professor was walking to the front of the room. It wasn't like I could tell him no without making a scene. Not to mention the fact I would be alerting him that his sexcapade bothered me.

"Sure," I replied, forcing a smile and focusing on the numbers the professor was writing on the board.

Did he have to sit so close? I could do without having to smell him. I was already aware he smelled delicious. I didn't need to be reminded.

"Are you going to look at me?" he asked.

No, dammit. I didn't want to look at him. I forced my head to turn and meet his gaze. He looked sad. I hadn't expected that. Why was he sad? I couldn't ask him that though. I wasn't going to let this thing go any further. I'd drawn my line. He would have to stay on his side. Which was to be my classmate and friend of a friend. Nothing more.

"Can we talk about it?" His voice was soft. He didn't want anyone else to hear him.

"Nothing to talk about. I need to listen to this if I'm gonna pass this class," I replied with the same fake smile.

"Pagan," he began and I held up a hand to stop him.

"If you want me to continue sitting here, then you'll stop now."

He nodded, "I'm sorry."

I hated the way he flinched when I spoke to him harshly. I just wanted him to go away. I didn't want to feel anything where he was concerned.

Class crept by at a snail's pace. When it was finally over, I didn't look at Dank. I'd successfully ignored him the entire class. Which had been easy considering he didn't say a word. I shoved my notebook into my bag and stood up. Dank was still sitting in his chair staring straight ahead with a deep frown on his ridiculously good looking face.

I should not care that he was upset. I should not care. I should not care. I kept chanting to myself as I walked down the aisle and toward the door. I would not look back. There was no reason to. The ache in my chest as I stepped out of the building leaving Dank sitting there alone like that bugged me. I rubbed the ball of my hand over my ache and kept going. I had a study group in thirty minutes.

* * * *

I hadn't expected to see Jay sitting on the steps of my dorm today. I wasn't really in the mood for it either, but perhaps he was here to pick up the redhead. I still didn't know her name. Could have her Dank had been screwing in the dark.

I smiled at Jay when his eyes met mine. He was a nice guy. At least he kept it real. He didn't act like he was just interested in you. He let you know he wasn't a one-woman kind of man. I had to respect that.

"Hello, Jay," I said as I reached the steps. I didn't figure I had to stick around for small talk.

Jay stood up blocking my path up the stairs, "Pagan, hey."

Okay, well, we'd said our polite greetings. I had assignments to work on. I started to step around him, but his hand reached out and took my hand. "Wait. I wanted to talk to you."

Well, crap. "'Bout what?" I asked, looking back up at the entrance so that he'd get the hint I had other things to get to.

"I know I screwed things up last week. I was an idiot. But you are all I've thought about for two weeks now. I can't get you out of my head. Please, just go have coffee with me. At least, let's be friends. I miss you."

Miranda was busy with Nathan all the time and now that I didn't have Dank hanging around, I was lonely. A friend would be nice. With Jay I knew where I stood. He was easy for me to read. No secrets, no sexy smoldering looks to give me the wrong idea.

"Friends would be good. I need a friend. Miranda spends more time on the UT campus with Nathan than she does here."

The big goofy grin I used to love broke out on Jay's face. "Can we go have coffee now? Or do you have a date with a textbook?"

The books could wait. "Let me go drop this thing off in my room and I'll be right back. Please feel free to ask out anyone who walks by that interests you," I teased.

Jay's frown appeared and I realized he didn't think it was funny. "It was a joke. If we're gonna be friends, then you have to relax," I said before opening the door and heading up to my room.

Once I reached my door, the sounds of moaning stopped me from turning the knob. I pressed my ear against the door and I heard Miranda cry out in obvious pleasure. Oh, wow. She was actually having sex with this guy. Backing away from the door, I went over to Gee's door and knocked softly.

Gee opened the door and reached up and pulled a cotton ball out of her ear. "What, you don't want to walk in on the porn show over there?" Gee asked.

"Not really, no. Could I leave my bag in here? Jay is waiting for me to go have coffee."

Gee scowled and nodded her head. She reached out and took the bag from my hands. "Yeah, fine." What was her problem? It was just my bag.

"How long have they been over there?" I asked looking toward my room where a grunt made me cringe. I could have done without hearing that.

"Long enough. They're rabbits. Fucking rabbits."

Poor Gee, stuck in here listening to them. "You want to go have coffee with me and Jay?"

Gee cocked her pierced eyebrow and shook her head, "No, thanks. I'm good. The cotton balls work."

"Okay, if you're sure."

Miranda's, "Oh, God," echoed down the hall. The girl was crazy. She was going to get caught. I walked over to our door and banged on it, "Put a sock in it, Miranda."

Gee shook her head and closed the door as I walked back by.

Jay was standing just outside the door waiting for me. He was also alone. Surprising. "Sorry that took so long. Miranda and Nathan are in our room—" I trailed off.

Nathan laughed, "Yeah, well, I'm just glad they moved it over here. I was getting tired of it."

"What? You mean this isn't the first time?"

Jay shook his head, "Nope. Not by a long shot."

I couldn't believe she was having wild loud sex with a guy she'd just met. No wonder she was gone all the time. She was in over her head way too fast. We were going to have to talk about this. The first relationship she had after Wyatt and she jumped into the physical part in less than two weeks.

"I had no idea."

Jay shrugged, "It happens. They are really into each other. Nathan talks about her nonstop. It may be a little early for the sex, but they both seem to be unable to keep their hands off each other."

"Yeah, I heard that. Several times," I mumbled.

Jay bumped my arm with his, "Don't worry about it, Pagan. Just be glad she's finally found life after Wyatt. And honestly, I've never seen Nathan that into someone before. He's normally disinterested."

That made it a little better, but still, in just two weeks?

"You still seeing Dank Walker?"

I rolled my eyes, "I was never seeing Dank Walker. We went out on one date. One. Then he was ready to move on to a new girl."

"Are you okay with that?" Jay asked, watching me for my reaction.

"Yes, I am. Like I said, it was just the one date. No big deal. I wasn't his type. You and I already knew that."

We reached Jay's little fancy sports car he'd gotten when he graduated from high school. I couldn't remember what it was called. I just knew he was in love with it. He walked me to my side and opened the door for me. I slid inside and he closed the door.

This was comfortable. I knew what to expect.

Chapter Eighteen

Dank

She wouldn't talk to me. I couldn't force her. I needed to win her trust. Dammit, I needed her to remember me. Remember *us*. Standing across the street, I watched as Jay bought her coffee and they sat down. They were like two old friends. It had been over a year since they broke up, yet there they sat laughing and talking like no time had passed. She'd forgiven him for being an ass, but she refused to talk to me. Was this what I'd been warned about? Was this when Pagan began to get feelings for Jay?

"She doesn't feel anything more than friendship and affection for him. You can see that from here," Gee said as she appeared beside me.

"I can only hope. She was so close to remembering. She was feeling things for me. Now, nothing. I can't get her to even speak more than one syllable words to me and that's if I'm lucky."

"This is the test, Dankmar. You knew it was coming. Her soul must have an opportunity to decide. When she is with you, she doesn't have a chance to do that because her feelings for you consume her even if she can't remember why. Her heart reacts to you. Her soul knows you."

My eyes burned. Pain sliced through me. She was mine. She owned me. But she hated me. How was I supposed to function like this? Right now, I had no chance at winning her heart or her soul.

"Stop standing around and being all wounded and shit. Go do something about it. You're Dank Walker. You're fucking Death. He's a human soul. You got this. Go figure it out."

Gee was always good for a pep talk. And she was right. I needed to get it together and find a way to get her back. I'd come to her like a human. Just another guy. I hadn't invaded her soul. I could reach places Jay couldn't.

"What if she never remembers?"

"Then you better make her fall in love with you, again."

"How did I do it the first time?"

"You let her in."

I let her in. She'd seen the real me. I hadn't been scared to show her who I was. I'd never hidden from her the fact that I wasn't human. She might not have known I was Death, but she'd thought I was a soul. This Pagan no longer saw lost souls who roamed the earth. The Voodoo lord of the dead's hold was no longer on her. That was forgotten. I'd treated her like someone else. Someone who could break. My Pagan was strong. She didn't hide from anything.

You're mine, Pagan Moore. You will always be mine.

I watched as she stopped listening to Jay and looked around her. I stepped forward out of the shade from the trees. Her eyes found me. I could see the confusion in them from here.

You own me. Once you knew this. I'm going to make sure you remember.

Pagan's coffee cup fell from her hands and the boy jumped up from the hot liquid now running off the side of the table. This was what I should have done all along. It was time I made sure Pagan understood I wasn't here for any other reason but her.

Pagan

Dank was talking in my head. How? I wasn't going crazy. I watched him across the street. He stood there and talked in my head. I couldn't concentrate on anything Jay said on the way back to the dorm. We both had coffee-stained clothing. We may even have some burns. All I'd been able to do was apologize. I couldn't manage more than that. Because Dank had talked in my head; he had spoken over my thoughts. It was his voice. I heard him loud and clear.

I stopped at Gee's door and knocked twice, but she didn't answer. Frustrated, I went to my room and started to open it, but then changed my mind and knocked first. I did not want to see Nathan's bare ass. No one answered. I unlocked the door and went inside. Miranda's bed was a mess and I decided I didn't want to think about that. I would focus on Dank Walker talking in my head. Was he a wizard? That sounded stupid even saying it. Was he into Voodoo because I'd heard Gee say something about Voodoo more than once. No, that didn't make any sense.

The door swung open and Miranda came in smiling from ear to ear.

"I am so freaking in love," she said with a happy sigh and closed the door behind her. Leaning back against it, she turned her bright, very pleased face my way.

"I'd say you are in lust since you just met the guy," I decided to be honest. She was delusional if she thought she was in love.

"Lust, love, it all goes together," she replied with a wave of her hand.

I knew for a fact that it did not all go together. I had experienced lust with Dank, but I'd never loved him. Had I?

"Sorry about earlier, but Pagan, you have no idea how good he is."

"Please stop right now! I do not want to hear the details of your sex life. I could hear it. I am very aware that you were enjoying yourself."

Miranda giggled and skipped over to her bed and fell face down on it and began smelling her pillow. "He is wonderful and he smells so good."

"Good to know." I replied.

"Oh, I heard you went to coffee with Jay. How'd that go?" Miranda asked, hugging the pillow to her chest.

"It went well until I dropped my coffee and spilled it all over both of us. I think I may end up with a blister on my hand. It burned me good."

Miranda covered her mouth, "Oh no! Did Jay get mad?"

I had no idea how Jay reacted because all I could think about was Dank…talking in my head. I couldn't exactly tell her that though. "He was startled and then he laughed. Not much else to it. We had to leave so we could both go home and change."

Miranda started laughing and couldn't stop. I had to grin because it was funny. I'd more than likely ruined Jay's shirt. I should probably offer to buy him a new one.

"They're having a party at the frat house tonight. I can bring anyone I want. Jay would love for you to come. Even if you did burn his body."

I didn't think facing Victoria at a frat party was something I wanted to tackle just yet. Besides, Jay and I were just friends and he'd end up with some girl and I'd be left alone to swat off drunken frat boys all night. Nope, not up for that. "I would rather just stay here. Get some more work done and go to bed early."

Miranda sighed and shook her head, "You are missing out on the fun things in college."

I'd tried having some college fun and it hadn't ended so well.

* * * *

Miranda was staying with Nathan after the party. This was more than likely going to become a trend. I didn't like being alone at night, but I figured Gee was right next door. I snuggled under the covers and closed my eyes. Just as I started to fall asleep, the strums of a guitar filled my room. I tried to open my eyes, but I couldn't. Panic started to set in. I wasn't asleep yet. Why wouldn't my eyes open?

It's just me, Pagan

Dank's voice was in my head again. I needed to open my eyes. Something was very wrong. Then he began singing the hauntingly familiar song that I'd heard at his concert. The song that had sent me into a panic attack. This time there was no fear. Just warmth.

"You weren't meant for the ice, you weren't made for the pain.
The world that lives inside of me brought only shame.
You were meant for castles and living in the sun. The cold running through me should have made you run.

Yet you stay. Holding onto me, yet you stay, reaching out a hand that I push away. Yet you stay. When I know it's not right for you. Yet you stay. Yet you stay.

I can't feel the warmth. I need to feel the ice. I want to hold it all in until I can't feel the knife. So I push you away and I scream out your name. I know I can't need you yet you give in anyway. Yet you stay. Holding onto me. Yet you stay reaching out a hand that I pushed away. Yet you stay. When I know it's not right for you. Yet you stay yet you stay.

I can't feel the warmth. I need to feel the ice. I want to hold it all in until I can't feel the knife. So I push you away and I scream out your name. I know I can't need you yet you give in anyway. Yet you stay. Holding onto me. Yet you stay reaching out a hand that I pushed away. Yet you stay. When I know it's not right for you. Yet you stay yet you stay.

Yet you stay holding onto me. Yet you stay, reaching out a hand that I pushed away. Yet you stay, when I know it's not right for you. Yet you stay.

Oh the dark will always be my cloak. And you are the threat to unveil my pain. So leave, leave and erase my memories. I need to face the life that was meant for me. Don't stay and ruin all my plans. You can't have my soul oh I'm not a man. The empty vessel I dwell in is not meant to feel the heat you bring so I push you away and I push you away, yet you stay. Oh, yet you stay, yet you stay.

Yet you stay."

Listen here: https://soundcloud.com/abbi-glines/yet-you-stya

Dank

I decided my human form was less helpful at the moment. I walked the campus following Pagan in my true form. The one only souls could see. The one Pagan had once been able to see. She'd slept deeply last night after I sang her to sleep. Not being able to snuggle up beside her and hold her had been hard, but she wasn't ready to accept me yet. I wouldn't do something she didn't welcome.

Pagan stopped outside the campus food court and looked around. Was she looking for me? I knew she wasn't looking for Jay.

Are you looking for me?

She stiffened, then gave a little nod of her head.

Meet me at the park across the street.

She didn't respond immediately, but she turned around to look at the park. A small nod followed. I watched her walk that way and fell in step behind her.

"Why can I feel you? Where are you?" She asked in a hushed whisper.

She could feel me behind her. I liked that. Her soul recognized me.

"I'm right here," I replied as I appeared beside her.

She jumped and let out a yelp. Then her startled expression turned into more of a pissed off glare. She picked up her pace and we were across the street and in the empty park in just a few more steps.

"What are you and why are you in my head and how did you sing to me last night and how did you just appear out of nowhere?" She stammered over her words. I knew she thought saying this out loud sounded insane.

"I'm not human. You knew that once."

Pagan threw up both her arms, "What the heck does that mean? You're not human? I used to know this? You've got to give me something that makes sense, Dank."

I wasn't handling this well.

"I know and if you give me a second, I will." I assured her and she put both hands on her hips and tilted her head to let me know she was waiting for more.

I couldn't tell her that her memory was gone. That was the only rule I had to follow. They never said I couldn't tell her I was Death. Well, maybe they had implied it, but they hadn't actually said it. They didn't think I'd be brave enough to tell her because it might put a hitch in my winning her love again. I was told I had to get her to fall in love with me again and choose me over her soul's mate. Those were the rules.

"The song I sang to you last night, the one that upset you at the concert," I took a step toward her and she tensed up, "can you tell me those words? Do you remember them?"

"Yet you stay?"

"Yes, but there are more words. Do you remember them? Any of them?"

I needed her to remember something. For something from our past to be restored. I'd sung that song to her wanting to remind her soul of what we'd had.

"You weren't meant for the ice. You weren't made for the pain. The world that lives inside of me brought only shame. You were meant for castles and living in the sun. The cold running through me should have made you run," she said the words slowly, trying to understand them.

"Yes. That's good. Do you remember any of the other words?"

She closed her eyes and shook her head, "I'm trying." Then her eyes flew open, "Don't stay and ruin all my plans. You can't have my soul. I'm not a man. The empty vessel I dwell in is not meant to feel the heat you bring. So I push you away and I push you away…yet you stay."

"Does any of that make sense to you?" I still held onto the hope that she would remember something.

"No. It's very sad and dark. None of it makes sense."

Sighing, I ran a hand through my hair. How was I supposed to explain this to her? "Do you know what a soul is, Pagan? I mean, really understand what a soul is?"

She scrunched up her nose. "Yeah, it's what is inside. It's who you are."

I nodded, "And a body is the house for the soul. Once the body dies, the soul is given another life."

"So you are one of those reincarnation believers?"

No, I wasn't a believer. I knew the facts. I shook my head, "No. I don't believe anything. I know. Your soul is who you are. In this body and in the next it is you. It will always be you. I don't get to have a soul, Pagan. This isn't a body. Not like yours. It is me. I can appear to humans and I can walk beside them invisible. I choose who will see me."

"You're like a…ghost? Because I'm not believing that. I touched you, I know you're very real."

Grinning for the first time since I'd started this conversation, I shook my head. "No, I'm not a ghost. I'm who comes to take the soul from the body. It is my job to take the soul from the body that can no longer house it. I send the soul on so that it can be given another body."

Pagan stood there studying me carefully. I could see her mind processing what I'd just told her. Calling myself something she'd said she hated wasn't what I wanted to do. I didn't want her to immediately hate me because of my title.

"I don't understand. What does that mean?"

"Oh, for crying the cuck out loud. I got to do this last time and I'm going to do it this time. It just sounds better coming from me," Gee announced as she walked out from behind a tree.

Pagan spun around to look at her. "Gee?"

"Yeah, Peggy Ann, it's me. Who else would be listening in on this crazy assed shit?"

"Gee, let me do this," I said, not wanting her here for this.

"You can't do this, Dankmar. You should have kept your mouth shut. But you couldn't. Now you've started this and you gotta finish it," Gee turned her focus to Pagan.

"We've already done this song and dance once, but I will tell you it was a helluva lot more fun the first time around. The drama was high and Dank's existence was on the line. This time, we don't have to worry about people dying and shit."

"Gee, leave," I demanded. But Gee was one of the few beings who didn't fear me.

"Sure thing. But first let me clear this up. Pagan, Dank's actual title in the great big scheme of things is Death. When it's your time to go, this is the guy who shows up."

Pagan took a step back from me, then another. She shifted her frightened gaze from me to Gee. I waited for her to argue or call Gee a liar. She didn't do either of those things.

"Say something, Pagan," I begged.

"Stay away from me," she demanded, then spun around and ran.

Chapter Nineteen

Pagan

I was afraid to sleep. Miranda was gone. Gee was…Gee was an old friend of Dank's. I jumped up and ran over to the bathroom door and locked it on my side. I went and locked my room door too. It wasn't that I didn't believe them. Dank had talked in my head, controlled my sleep, and appeared out of nowhere. He was something. Accepting that he was Death was easier than thinking he was something like a ghost or wizard or, God forbid, a vampire. Those were mythical creatures. They weren't real. But Death, Death was real.

Could Death be more than just the time a body dies? The soul has to let go. Is death called what it is because of the one who takes the soul? It made sense. I believed him. And I was equally terrified of him. It wasn't healthy for a human to have a relationship with Death. He was the end-all. I wasn't ready to die. I didn't want to see him again until it was my time to go. I hoped I wouldn't be until I was very old and wrinkly.

A knock on the bathroom door startled me and I grabbed the nearest tool I could find. A pencil sharpener. Not very threatening.

"Open the door, Peggy Ann, or I'm coming in. It's really easy for me."

Was she Death too? Were there more of them? Did they all sing in rock bands or dress emo?

"Fine. I'm not gonna beg," Gee said as she appeared in my room.

"What are you?" I asked scooting back on my bed, holding my pencil sharpener in front of me.

"What you gonna do? Peg me with a pencil sharpener? Really?" Gee shook her head in disbelief and walked over and sat on the end of Miranda's bed, then jumped back up again. "I forgot about the action this thing has been getting lately. I think I'll stand."

"Please, just go away," I begged.

"First, I need you to ask me about all those crazy-ass things you have going through your head. You won't talk to Dank, so talk to me."

"Are you a death too?" I asked, because I had to know if I should be praying for my soul and digging out those rosary beads of Miranda's.

"Death is one being. Dankmar is Death. He has been and will forever be."

"Why do you call him Dankmar?"

"It's his name. Dankmar means 'famous for his spirit'. It fits. He used to only have the name Death. An old Irish lady gave it to him right before her soul's departure. She said he deserved a name more fitting."

His name meant something? Why did that tug at me? He was Death, for crying out loud. "Why is he a lead singer in a band?"

Gee cackled with laughter, "That's a damn good question. Even Death gets bored. Every few decades, he becomes something different. It all started in the first century when he became a gladiator. The list is long, but the ones that amused me most were when he was a pirate in the 1500s, an outlaw in the 1800s, and in the 1920s he was a gangster. He found a music that appealed to him in the early eighties. So now, when Death isn't taking souls, he's a singer in a rock band. However, one time not too long ago, he was putting an end to that one too. He had something else that filled his time. That has changed recently."

"So Death just walks the earth? He has no other dwelling?" I was having a hard time wrapping my head around this.

"Yep. He just fills his limited free time with hobbies."

"Then what are you?"

"I'm a transporter. I take the soul once Dankmar takes it from the body. I take it up or down. Whichever way it's going. The ones that go up get another life. It's pretty simple. Humans try to make it more complicated than it is. The Creator doesn't make new souls often. Only when so many bad ones have come through and he needs to replace them with good ones. For example, you're a new soul."

I was a new soul. How strange. People lived their entire lives not knowing if they had past lives. Not knowing if they would get another. But I now knew this was my first chance. My first experience. There was no past for me. This was it—I only had a future.

"Is it my time to go? Is that why you and Dank are near me? Are you going to take my soul soon?" That was my biggest fear. I didn't want to die. Surely, if this was my first life, I would get more than just eighteen short years.

"Nope, Peggy Ann. Your time isn't up. I would be willing to bet you're the only human alive that has an unlimited lifespan."

"What?"

Gee waved me off, "Nothing, forget I said that. Just rest assured we aren't here to take you. However, Dank is captivated by you. That doesn't put you in danger. If he were to take your soul, he wouldn't get to keep it. He would lose it. The Creator would then take it. So, you are in no danger."

I sat there letting all this information process in my head. I didn't question it. This made sense. It was crazy as hell, but it made sense. I felt complete peace about it. But there was one thing I wanted to make very clear. I lifted my eyes to meet Gee's, "I do not want to see Dank again. Having Death as an acquaintance is not normal. I realize I'm not in danger, but I want to be left alone. I want to date boys who can't talk in my head and take souls from bodies. I'd like someone who isn't immortal. Dank is hard to resist. He's hard to push away. If he stayed near me, I'd cave in and let him closer. I don't want that. So, please, go."

Gee didn't reply. She didn't have a witty comeback or smart remark. After a few seconds, I looked up and she was gone. No goodbye. No Gee. And no more Dank.

Dank

I'd gambled and lost.

Gee sat quietly beside me. She'd done what I'd asked her to. Pagan had made her choice. Even before she knew there was a choice to make. I would never be in the running. She didn't want me near her. She didn't want to see me again. I wouldn't be able to walk this world unless I was working. I couldn't deal with knowing she was here and I couldn't talk to her. Touch her. Slipping the necklace she had given me from around my neck, I held it in my hands tightly. This was all I had of Pagan—the Pagan who had loved me, who had accepted me for what I was, and had wanted me anyway. I couldn't exist with any reminder of her. I had to leave my memories behind. I had to remember who I was and what I was meant to do. No more living in the human world.

Pagan's room was dark and her slow even breathing told me she was sleeping. I walked over to her desk and quietly placed the necklace she'd once wanted me to have because it symbolized her unending love, on top of her notebook. It was hers. I couldn't keep it, but I couldn't let anyone else have it either. This was Pagan's. This was one memory of me that I could leave with her. I walked over to stand beside her bed for the last time. I allowed myself to watch her sleep. From the moment I'd first seen her, I'd been watching her sleep. It was a peacefulness I only experienced with her. She'd taught me that I was capable of love. She taught me to laugh. She taught me what it meant to cherish something or someone completely. I would move on and leave her to this life, but what we had would always be there reminding me of the beauty I once had. When it came time for her soul to leave this body, I would have to find the strength to let the only memory of me she would have be lost forever.

"Goodbye, Pagan Moore," I whispered into the darkness then bent down to press a kiss to her lips.

CHAPTER TWENTY

Pagan

Sleeping on it didn't make it any easier to accept. It seemed like a really bad dream. I rolled over to see Miranda's empty bed. Another night with Nathan. I had two female friends here. One was in heat and always gone. The other wasn't human. I was truly alone. I reached for my phone and scrolled down my contacts until I found my mother's number. I needed to hear her voice. This must be what homesickness felt like.

"Pagan? Hey, honey, are you okay?"

"I'm okay," I assured her. I wasn't one to call home much. The one time we had talked last week had been when she'd called me to see how I was settling in.

"It's seven in the morning. I didn't realize you were capable of being awake at seven in the morning."

"Ha. Ha. I have three eight a.m. classes a week, thank you very much."

"Oh, well, that explains it. This is a new phenomenon. I normally had to beat you with your bacon in the mornings to get you up before seven thirty."

"I'm a big girl now," I replied, feeling a lump form in my throat. Talking to mom wasn't making this better. I wanted to go curl up on the couch with her and watch CSI reruns.

"You sure? Because something sounds wrong."

"I miss you," I managed to choke out without crying.

"Oh, baby. I miss you too. Are you homesick? I could come visit. Do you want me to come visit?"

No. I didn't want her to come visit because I may not let her leave me. "No. I'm fine. I just wanted to hear your voice this morning and tell you that I miss your pancakes. A caramel latte just isn't the same thing."

Mom chuckled into the phone. "Well, as soon as you get home for Thanksgiving break, I will have pancakes waiting for you."

"Thanks. I can look forward to those. I need to go now. I've got to get dressed."

"Alright. Don't be late for class. Call me anytime you want to. You're a beautiful, smart girl and you'll find your place there real soon."

"Okay, I'll talk to you soon. Love you."

"Love you, honey. Bye.

"Bye."

I dropped the phone onto the bed and stood up to go get a shower. My eyes landed on the silver Celtic knot that had once hung around Dank's neck. It was lying on top of my notebook. I started to reach for it, but stopped. I wasn't sure how it got here or why it was here. I'd told him to leave me alone. I didn't like thinking he could be in my room while I was sleeping. I hurried to the bathroom. Getting out of this room and in the real world where people had bodies and weren't immortal was one and only goal.

* * * *

When I opened the front door of the dorm to head to class, I stopped when Jay shoved off from the railing he had been leaning on. He had a coffee in his hand. I knew Jay didn't drink coffee.

"Good morning," he said smiling and holding the coffee out toward me. "Caramel latte with whipped cream."

"Thank you," I replied, taking the cup from him. "What did I do to deserve morning coffee service?"

Jay shrugged, "It gave me a reason to see you. Miranda told me what time you left this morning and I thought I'd see if I could score some brownie points. The fact I get to start my day with you was also a pretty big draw."

Smiling, I took a sip of the coffee, then sighed my approval. "Well, thank you. That's really sweet."

"I had one more ulterior motive," he said and rubbed his hands together. That was his nervous gesture. I knew it well.

"Okay, but can we discuss it on my way to class so I'm not late?" I asked, stepping up beside him.

"Yeah, yeah, of course." We walked down the stairs and headed for the sidewalk that led to the front of the English building.

"Okay. What is it you want that you got up to come bribe me with coffee this early in the morning?"

"I was wondering if there was any chance you'd give me one more chance at a date. Just friends, but, well, not just as friends. I want to spend time with you. Maybe we could go out to eat and then bowling. You used to kick my tail at bowling."

Under normal circumstances, this would have been a definite no. However, I was lonely. I needed friends. Jay had been my friend for several years. Spending time with him wasn't the worst idea in the world. Hanging out with Death was the worst idea in the world. This was definitely a step up—at least he was human. He wasn't as sexy and his kisses didn't make my toes curl, but he was nice enough. I couldn't measure other guys against Dank. It was unfair. He wasn't human so therefore a human could not compete.

"Sure. That sounds like fun. When do you want to do this?"

Jay stopped walking and looked over at me as if he didn't believe I'd just said yes. He started walking again grinning like I'd just offered him money instead of agreeing to go on a date with him. "Uh, tomorrow night. We don't have school the next morning."

Sure. I needed something to do. "Sounds like a plan."

* * * *

Three weeks later and I'd found a comfortable pattern with Jay. He brought me coffee three days a week and walked me to class. We went out to eat with Miranda and Nathan on Tuesdays, we went bowling on Thursdays, and Friday nights was dinner and a movie. It was exactly like high school. Everything was very organized and very predictable.

The one thing I'd learned, however, was that having someone with you all the time did not take away the loneliness. You could be surrounded by people and still feel lonely. Something was missing. I could almost pinpoint it, but right when it was within my grasp, I'd forget. It just slipped away.

Tonight, I was supposed to go to a study group for my Literature class that Dank was no longer in. It bothered me that I missed him. I shouldn't miss him. The excitement of walking into class knowing he might be there was gone now. I had the excitement of a well planned out relationship. I grabbed my book bag and headed out the door and down the steps. The loud screeching of metal and horns blaring stopped me. Then the twisting, crunching sound of metal against metal filled the air. People began pouring out of the dorm to see what had happened. I walked with the crowd closer to the street where the two cars that had collided were now still. Smoke was streaming out of the hoods. The smaller car was upside down. I heard people screaming to call 911. Others were crying.

The shattering of glass drew everyone's attention to the car that had flipped. The weight the SUV was putting on the windows must have been too much. No one was moving in either car. I heard girls on their phones around me making phone calls and telling other people about the wreck. No one seemed to know who it was just yet.

It was then that I felt him. I couldn't see him, but he was here. No one else seemed to notice. Why was it that I did? I scanned both the wrecked cars for any signs of him, but he wasn't visible. The fact I knew he was nearby didn't frighten me at all. If I was honest with myself, I wanted to see him. Warmth ran up my arms and I shivered. "Where are you?" I whispered.

I got no response.

The warmth only lasted a short time and then it was gone. Sirens began to blare and the crowd was moved back. I was numb.

He'd gone.

I was sad. Not only because I knew someone in those cars had died. I was also sad because he'd been close, but I hadn't been able to see him. Why would I want to see him? Was something wrong with me?

I pushed my way back through the crowd until I was free of the bodies pressed closely together as they tried to get a closer look at the accident. Taking a deep breath, I walked over and sat down on the steps. I was positive that our study group would not meet tonight. I just hoped it was no one I knew in those vehicles.

My phone began ringing and I pulled it out to see Miranda's number flashing on the screen.

"Hey."

"Oh, my god. Thank goodness you're okay. I just saw the wreck on the news and it was right outside our dorm. They aren't releasing any more information, so I wasn't sure. Jay is already on his way over there. I called him and he left work and headed your way."

I wasn't in the mood for Jay tonight. I wanted to go curl up in my room alone and pull out the necklace I'd hidden in my drawer. Dank had left it with me for a reason. I needed to understand why.

"I'm fine. I'm not sure they'll let him through. I think they have roads blocked off. But I'll call and let him know I'm safe. It is a bad one. No one knows who it is yet."

"Call me as soon as you find out and you go inside and be safe," Miranda said in a commanding voice. Smiling, I agreed and hung up.

By the time Jay arrived, the cars were being towed off the road and the coroner had pronounced the driver of the smaller car dead and the body had been taken away. The passenger of the other vehicle had also been pronounced dead. All I could think about was that Dank had to live through this daily. It was something he could never escape. Did it bother him? Was there any emotion involved for him?

"Here, I brought you something to eat," Jay said as he climbed the steps to the dorm and sat beside me. I hadn't been able to walk away from the accident. I'd been sitting here watching it. Every moment. Every sob and wail of family members arriving at the scene to be told someone they loved was dead. I'd watched it all. They walked away tonight hating death. It had taken from them. I could understand their pain, but my chest ached for Dank. He didn't cause the accident. He didn't choose to have those people die. It was their bodies that couldn't survive. It wasn't his fault that their souls could no longer stay inside those bodies. But because of his name and his purpose, people hated him. This unavoidable event in everyone's life wasn't an event at all. It was a being. If they only understood that it wasn't Death's fault at all.

"I figured you hadn't eaten anything," Jay said as I took the bag from him. The smell of a greasy hamburger and even greasier fries wafted up from the bag. He was right. I hadn't eaten anything, but my stomach wasn't strong enough for food.

"I don't think I can eat anything," I said apologetically. It was nice of him to have thought of me, but tonight, I just wanted to go to bed and forget. Forget what I knew. Forget what I'd seen. It all hurt too much.

"You need to eat something. Come on, let's go inside. Watching this isn't good for you."

I shook my head. I had to stay until it was finished. I couldn't walk away just yet. "You can't go inside this late. It's past the curfew for guys to go inside. We should just stay right here."

Jay reached over and took my hand in his. There was no instant rush of pleasure or excitement. He didn't make my body react in any way. He was just my friend.

CHAPTER TWENTY-ONE

Dank

"I'm sick of the mopey shit. It is getting old. You can't mope for the rest of eternity. Especially, when you didn't even fight for her. You drop the bomb on her that you end human life and then you expect her to accept you with open arms. This ain't a damn soap opera."

I paced back and forth outside Pagan's dorm. It was three in the morning and I'd just finished my rounds. Seeing her tonight had made it impossible not to come back here when I was done.

"You know I'm right. She balked and hurt your feelings and you did the dark broody thing and left. Men are all the same."

"Shut up, Gee. I don't know what you expect me to do. She didn't want to ever see me again. I was giving her what she wanted."

Gee made a gagging sound. "No, you were being a big baby. Poor Dank can't get Pagan to remember him, so he tucks his tail and runs. Her soul mate thanks you. He really does. Now he doesn't have anything standing in his way."

"That's enough, Gee."

"Whatev, you need to grow a pair. She asked where you were tonight. I know you heard her. Hell, I heard her, and I wasn't the one pawing all over her. She wanted to see you then."

I stopped pacing and looked up at the window where I knew she was sleeping. I'd said my goodbye. I'd given her a normal life just like she wanted. Had it been the wrong thing to do? If I had pushed her to remember, if I had tried harder to make her love me, would it have worked?

"This is the unfair bitch of it all. She loves you. She just can't remember. Not because her mind is sick, or her brain is damaged, but because the Deity took that memory from her. Even though her head can't remember, her heart does."

I leaned against the brick wall and stared up at the dark sky. Would her heart win out? Could her heart trigger her memory to come back? What if she remembered one day and I was gone? What then? Did I just lose her forever and have her think I didn't want her? That I didn't love her?

"What do I do, Gee?"

"You fucking fight is what you do. You fucking fight."

"I don't want to destroy her. I don't want to hurt her. I just want her happy."

"She'll never be happy if she never remembers you."

Pagan

The door across the hall from mine was wide open when I stepped into the hall. A girl with tight black curls and an olive complexion was sitting on the bed talking to Janet, who shared that room with a girl name Tabby. The girl with curls waved at me and jumped up and ran to the door.

"Hey, we've not met yet. I'm Babes and yes, like for real, that is my name, please do not ask. My mother smoked a lot of pot. Janet said you shared this room with your friend Miranda who is never here."

She sure knew a lot about me. Janet stuck her head around the corner and her hair was up in a towel. "Morning, Pagan. Sorry about Babes and her morning chattiness. It can cause headaches."

Babes rolled her brown eyes and beamed up at me. Not many people were shorter than me, but Babes was barely five foot. Her mom's pot smoking must have stunted her growth.

"Are you going to the Omega party tonight?"

Shaking my head, I admitted, "I have no idea what that is." I wasn't a social bug. Just recently I'd been getting to know the other girls in my dorm.

"Ooooh, you have to go. The Omegas throw the best parties. They only let in attractive females. You'd get in, no problem."

No, thanks. I'd turned Jay down to all the ones he'd asked me to go to. I just couldn't bring myself to participate. It didn't sound like anything I was interested in.

"She's gonna say no. She never goes anywhere except with the cutie that shows up to get her a few times a week." Janet said from the chair she was sitting in brushing her hair.

"Oh, come on. It'll be fun. We can laugh at the insaneness together."

I was going to be late to class. "I'll think about it," I said walking down the hall.

"It was nice meeting you," she called out behind me.

She was a bubbly sort. "You too," I replied and hurried toward the door before she could say anything else. I definitely needed coffee before I could handle her again.

I expected Jay to be outside waiting on me with a cup of coffee in his hand. But for the first time in weeks, he wasn't. I had enough time to stop by the coffee house on my way to class if I hurried.

"Sleeping too late, Peggy Ann, tsk tsk tsk."

I stopped and spun around at the sound of Gee's voice. She was sitting on the hood of her little red sports car.

"Gee?"

She rolled her eyes, "Last time I checked."

I walked toward her, "What are you doing here?"

"I have something that belongs to you. I thought I'd bring it back. If I recall correctly, you were real attached to it."

What was she talking about? I was beside her car when she reached into her pocket and pulled something out and held out her hand. Slowly she opened it and nestled in the palm of her hand was a small gold brooch. It was a heart shaped filigree with pale pink stones. I'd seen this before. My heart pounded in my chest as I reached out and touched it.

"What is this?" I asked, lifting my gaze from the brooch to Gee's curious expression.

"I think you know. You should know. Why don't you take this brooch and put it in your pocket. Think about it. See if a memory doesn't find its way back inside."

I picked up the delicate brooch. It looked old, but well cared for. My head started to spin as I held it. She was right. There was a memory here.

"Where did you get it?

"Why, it's a funny thing you should ask me that. I found it in your room. Right where you left it."

How had she found this in my room? I didn't remember ever putting this anywhere in my room. I looked back up at her to ask, but she was gone.

I ran the pad of my thumb over the stones.

"Can you take this and give it to me after my soul leaves my body? I want to keep it."

A sharp pain sliced through my head. I reached out and grabbed the side of the car to keep from falling.

"I gave you this brooch. I told you that I wanted to take it with me. You said that could be arranged and you slipped it into your pocket"

Another hot blaze rocketed through my head. I sank down to the cement below. What was happening? There were memories attached to this brooch. Things I'd forgotten. I dropped the brooch into my lap and grabbed my head with both hands as the pain grew stronger.

"But you never saw me again. Because your soul was erased off the charts. The only reason I remembered you was because of this brooch."

"Aaaaaah!" I cried out in agony. With each memory that surfaced, the pain in my head grew stronger.

"So, I came to watch you. To see what was so unique about this soul."

I knew him. Dank. Oh, God. I knew him. Tears blurred my vision as I curled up in a ball on the hard ground. No one could see me tucked away between two cars. I bit my lip to keep from making any more sounds as the memories laced through my mind one sentence at a time. Each touch. Each moment. I'd forgotten it all. A sob escaped me and I fought back the wail growing in my chest. How had I forgotten him? I loved him. He was everything to me. How could I forget him? I'd sent him away. The sobs grew louder and I gave up trying to keep quiet. Between the shattering of my heart and the explosion in my head, I was unable to do little more than wither on the ground and weep.

CHAPTER TWENTY-TWO

Dank

The room was dark when I arrived. Gee had called me here. All she'd said was, "It's Pagan." I'd come immediately, but I hadn't expected it to be Pagan's dorm room she was calling me to. I scanned the room and found Pagan curled up on the bed asleep. It wasn't even lunchtime yet. The curtains were closed and the lights were off. Was she sick?

"She remembered," Gee said from the corner of the room where she sat watching me.

"What exactly did she remember?" I asked, taking a step toward the bed where Pagan was sleeping.

"Everything, I think. Hell, I don't know. She hasn't talked. I don't know how affected she is yet. If she's hurt, mentally, I expect you to extinguish me. I can't live with the guilt."

Panic gripped me and I rushed to the side of the bed and knelt down beside her. What had Gee done? She wasn't supposed to remember everything until the Deity decided it was time. I had been hoping for some small memory to come back to her, but never had I wanted to harm her.

"What…Did…You…Do?" I lifted my gaze from Pagan's still pale body and glared at Gee.

"Get mad. Please. I want you to. If she is messed up because I made a stupid ass decision, I'm not going to be able to live with it."

Gee's solemn expression didn't help. Gee was never serious. I reached up and brushed the hair from her face gently. The natural pink color of her cheeks was gone. "Tell me what you did, Gee," I begged. I couldn't help her if I didn't know what had happened. I needed an explanation.

"You weren't fighting. You were just letting her go. Fuck that. I wasn't going to let you go down so easily. She isn't happy with the so-called soul mate they created for her. She is lost without you. I…I gave her the brooch."

The brooch. The one I'd kept for her. The one I'd given back to her only last Valentine's Day. She'd remembered the time I'd come to her as a child. It had been her grandmother's. She'd wanted me to keep it for her and give it back to her in her next life. But she hadn't died then. The brooch had made me remember her name. So, when Pagan Moore was once again in the books to die, I remembered her. I went to see her. I was curious. And then it had become something more. So much more.

"What happened?" I asked, afraid to take my eyes off her. I wanted to will her awake. Make sure everything was okay. That her mind hadn't suffered a trauma too serious for her body to bear.

"I left her with it. Then I got worried and turned around and came back. She was…she was curled up on the cement with tears running down her face, saying, 'I forgot him. How could I forget him?' I carried her up here and she hasn't moved or said anything since. She just sleeps."

I couldn't deal with Gee right now. I didn't want her near me. "Go. Just go," I said without looking at her.

"You'll tell me if she wakes up, right? I need to know she's okay."

"I said to leave, Gee. You've done enough. Leave. Us."

She didn't argue. She was gone.

I reached for Pagan's hand and held it in mine. It was cold to the touch. I saw her soul. It wasn't damaged. Her body wasn't sick. This was all mental. I brought her hand to my lips and kissed it softly. I shouldn't have trusted Gee. I'd known she was going to do something stupid when she'd demanded I fight last night. I just hadn't thought she'd do something this detrimental. I had been working on a plan. Another one—one that might have actually worked. I had gone about making her fall in love with me again all wrong. I was going to fix that. I was also going to make sure she knew I had never had sex with some other girl. I wanted that cleared up. I didn't like that tainting us.

Pagan's hand moved in mine and I stilled. I waited to see if it happened again. Was she waking up? Could she wake up? Her hand barely squeezed mine and I watched it desperately hoping for more. After a few minutes, it hadn't moved again. I lifted my eyes to stare at her face. Her eyelids appeared blue. She was too pale.

I needed to do something. I'd gone weeks without holding her. She hadn't wanted me to. But now, I needed it. I needed Pagan safely in my arms. I couldn't sit here while she lay curled up in a ball, cold and pale. All I could do was wait and keep her warm.

I slipped off my boots and pulled back the cover before sliding in behind her. She immediately rolled toward me and her hands fisted in my shirt. She let out several small sighs then stilled once again.

Pagan

I was warm. Very warm and something smelled wonderful. I buried my face into the warmth. The smell grew stronger. I pressed closer to it and ran my hands up to get handfuls to bring it closer.

"Please tell me this means you're okay," a deep voice whispered in the darkness. The warmth was talking. I fought hard to open my eyes. They were so heavy.

"That's my girl, open those eyes and look at me," the voice said again. I knew that voice. Panic laced through me and I reached out and grabbed him. He was leaving me. I'd forgotten. I told him to go. I didn't know, I didn't know. I fought to open my eyes and reached frantically for a way to hold him here. When I opened my eyes, would he be gone?

"Shhh, it's okay. I have you. Easy, baby," he soothed me and his arms were around me, pulling me close to him.

My eyes finally opened and I stared at the chest I was pressed up against. I inhaled deeply. This was Dank. My Dank. This was my Dank.

He was here. Oh, thank God, he was here. I pushed back until I could look up at him.

"You're here," my voice sounded scratchy.

"Yeah, I'm here," he replied. His blue eyes glowed in the darkness. I knew that glow. I also knew they would glow brighter after he took a soul.

"Don't leave," I begged, tightening my hold on the tee shirt I held in my hands.

"I won't," he assured me, then he looked me in the eyes. "Do you remember?"

Yes. I remembered everything. The last two months replayed in my head. Those two weeks with Dank. He'd been himself and I'd not remembered anything. He'd tried so hard to reach me. Wait…the girl…the library.

"Explain the girl outside the library," I said needing to hear an explanation because I knew there had to be one. My Dank would never do that.

"There's this…guy who you won't remember, but he believes I took you from him. So, he set it up to make you hate me. He wanted me to lose you too. He knew you weren't yourself and he took advantage of it."

"Leif?"

Dank's eyes widened in surprise. "Yeah, Leif, but Pagan…you aren't supposed to be able to remember him. He doesn't have a soul."

Because he was a Voodoo spirit. "I know that, but I remember him."

Dank brushed the hair back from my face and smiled. "You never did fit the mold. I've missed you so much."

The relief and love in his eyes made me tear up. I'd treated him so badly. "I'm so sorry. I love you, Dank. I love you so much. I don't know what happened. I can't believe I forgot you."

Dank lowered his mouth and pressed a kiss to my forehead, "Don't apologize. It's okay. You had nothing to do with this. It is the Deity that did this. They took your memories."

Why? What had I done wrong?

"Did I make them mad?"

Dank shook his head and tightened his hold on me. I realized my hands were still fisting handfuls of his shirt and I released them and smoothed his shirt out.

"When a soul is created, so is it's mate. Jay is your soul's mate. You weren't created to be my mate. You have to reconnect with Jay and let your soul decide if you can live without him. They took your memories to make the choice fair. I don't know how you remembered without their help. But we can't let them know. You will have to continue the way we were. They want you to choose and now the choice is no longer fair. I don't want them to take your memories again."

They could take them again? No. No. I didn't want that. "So, I do what? Date Jay? I don't want to date Jay."

Dank flashed a small smile, then lowered his mouth to mine, "I don't want that either, but I can't lose you again. I need you to remember me."

His mouth covered mine and I decided right now that wasn't the most important thing. This was. I slipped my hands into his hair and pulled him closer. The first taste of his tongue was heavenly. I rolled onto my back and tugged at his hair pulling him on top of me. I wanted to be covered with him. I needed him close. I'd kept him at a distance because my stupid mind had betrayed me. Dank shifted and moved his body until it fit perfectly over mine. His arms rested on each side of my head as he held some of his weight off me. I didn't want that. I wanted all of him. Opening my legs caused his hips to fall against me.

He stopped himself from fully pressing into me. I pulled back from the kiss, "Please, Dank. Don't hold yourself off me."

He swallowed hard then slowly lowered his hips until his arousal pressed firmly against me. Whimpering a little from the new sensation, I rocked against him. His lips were on mine again instantly and his tongue was stroking the inside of my mouth with a frenzied need. I rocked again and let out a small cry of pleasure as the tingling between my legs shot sparks throughout my body.

Dank let out a groan as our tongues tangled with each other and this time it was his hips that rocked against mine. The pressure was more intense. I threw back my head and let out a sound I'd never made before. Dank's lips began trailing kisses down my exposed neck and stopped at my collar bone. Then the rough skin from his fingertips touched the sensitive skin just under the bottom of my shirt. I began panting, hoping he didn't stop. His hand crept up further until his hand found the snap between my breasts and undid my bra easily. He pushed the unwanted barrier away before running his fingers over each nipple.

"Do you want me to stop?" he asked in a raspy whisper.

I shook my head.

"I want your shirt off," he said, watching me for a reaction.

"Okay," I replied, leaning up to take it off.

"No, I want to take it off," he said, stopping me.

I nodded and he lifted the shirt up and over my head. His hands pushed the straps of my bra back until I had nothing covering me.

"You're beautiful," he whispered.

His praise made my heart soar.

"I think I remember telling you'd I'd like to see you with your shirt off," I reminded him.

A smirk appeared on his sexy full lips and he reached for the hem of his shirt and pulled it over his head.

Oh my.

I reached out and ran my fingers over each defined ab muscle. Now, that was beautiful. "Come here," I said lying back against the pillow again.

Dank's eyelids were lowered and he gazed hungrily down at me. I wanted his bare chest pressed against mine. Reaching up, I slipped my hands behind his head and brought him all the way down until I could taste his lips. His chest brushed against mine and I bit down on his bottom lip causing an approving groan to erupt from Dank as the intimate touch of our bodies brought us closer together.

This was my Dank. I didn't feel lost or lonely anymore. That feeling had engulfed me over the past few weeks, but I understood it now. My heart had known it had been missing Dank.

CHAPTER TWENTY-THREE

Dank

Pagan hadn't wanted to put our shirts back on once I'd finally put a halt to things. When she'd slipped her hand between my legs, I was pretty sure I was going to blow. She'd just gotten her memory back. She wasn't ready for that yet. We'd gone further tonight sexually than we ever had before. I wanted to ease her into things and not rush her. However, Pagan's slow, even breaths caused her chest to rise and press against mine, causing friction that I couldn't ignore. Each time her little erect nipples rubbed against my skin, I had to take deep calming breaths.

"Well, it looks like she's gonna make it. Memory intact and all," Gee's voice surprised me. I hadn't expected her back tonight. I pulled the blanket up over us.

"Yeah, thanks. Not exactly something I want to see. So, do you think you could have, oh, I don't know, let a girl know something? I've been worried sick since I left here."

"Shhhh...don't wake her up. She's tired."

"I just bet she is. She wakes up to wild hot sex with Death. She needs her rest."

"That didn't happen. Shut up," I warned her quietly so not to disturb Pagan.

Gee rolled her eyes, "Yeah, right."

"She has her memory back. She's fine. Now go."

Gee winked and was gone.

"You should be nicer to her," Pagan whispered against my chest.

Damn it, Gee. She'd woken her up.

"I'm sorry. Go back to sleep."

Pagan tilted her head back and smiled up at me sheepishly, "Well, I would, but I think we may need to put our shirts on. Waking up to this makes me want to do…things."

Knowing she wanted to do things made me throb harder. I was going to have to get up and take a cold shower. "Yeah, probably a good idea."

Pagan pushed against me and rolled over on top of me. She straddled me and placed both her hands on my shoulders. "Or we could do things."

Pagan sitting on top of me with her hair falling down over her shoulders topless looking like a goddess was something no man could turn down.

"What things do you want to do?" I asked as I reached up and brushed her nipple with my thumb.

"I want to take off our bottoms," she whispered and dropped her gaze to my stomach.

Oh damn. I was a goner.

"Pagan, if we take off our pants, things could go further…"

She lifted her eyes back up to meet mine and tilted her head to the side, grinning playfully. "I know. I want to go further. With you. I want to reassure myself that I didn't lose you. That you're here. I need that. Right now."

All the reasons this was a bad idea ran through my head as she crawled off me and began taking off her shorts. The light blue lace panties that were left had my complete attention. She slipped her fingers under the waistband of her panties, but stopped before she pulled them down. Why did she stop? I tore my eyes from her lacy underwear to meet her gaze.

She licked her lips nervously, "I've never been naked in front of someone before," she admitted.

"Good," I replied, sitting up and reaching for her waist and pulling her to me. "You don't have to get naked in front of me now if you aren't ready. But if you want to, then I will be a very, very happy man."

Pagan laughed softly, "Actually, you'll be a very, very happy Death."

I took a nip at her earlobe, then whispered, "That's right and right now Death has very, very naughty thoughts about you. So, please take off those sexy panties and crawl back in this bed with me."

Pagan shivered in my arms, "That sure is a good way to ask."

She moved back and slowly pulled them down her legs, inch by inch, until she was completely naked. My restraint was shot. I stood up and grabbed her and laid her back on the bed before quickly getting out of my jeans and covering her body with mine.

I never once took my eyes off Pagan's face. Through each new touch and experience, I watched her. The sounds and looks of ecstasy on her face were getting locked away for me to remember forever. This was only the first time, but it was a moment I would never forget. It was sacred.

Pagan

Dank and I made love for the first time and the second and the third before Miranda knocked on the door. Dank kissed me and disappeared before I got up and opened it for her. She'd lost her key two weeks ago and we still couldn't find it.

"What have you been doing? I've called you and texted you. Jeez, girl, you're hard to get in touch with."

Miranda walked in going on and on about Nathan being a jerk. I couldn't concentrate on what she was saying because the realization of who Nathan was hit me. I grabbed the doorknob to keep from falling.

"Are you listening to me?" Miranda asked. "Are you sick, Pagan? Because you look like you're about to pass out."

Go sit on the bed. It's okay. I know what you're remembering.

Dank was still in here. I nodded for his benefit and walked over to the bed and sat down. "I'm good. Just got dizzy. You woke me up."

Miranda frowned and plopped down beside me. "You sure?"

"Yes, I'm positive."

"Well, then should I forgive him?"

Forgive who? Nathan? I was confused.

"Could you explain all that again? The dizzy thing kind of made it hard to understand what you were saying."

And yes, you should forgive Nathan because he is Wyatt. I couldn't say that, of course. But now I wanted to go hug Nathan and tell him how much I had missed him. He'd think I'd lost my mind. No wonder I liked him so much.

"This Siera girl. She calls him to come change her light bulb at six in the morning and he goes, Pagan. He up and goes to fix her light. She isn't an idiot. She can fix it herself. Why would he go do that? I don't understand him. We had amazing hot sex last night and I wake up to a note from him saying he'd be right back, that Siera called, that her light was out and she needed help changing it."

That was weird. Nathan needed to be slapped around a little.

"You have every right to be upset. But maybe you misunderstood him."

Miranda shrugged and laid her head over on my shoulder. "I don't think you can misunderstand that. Guys suck. But you know that. You really liked Dank and he went and screwed that girl. Then Jay bores you. I can see it all over your face. Also, I think he may be screwing Victoria again, just so you know."

Good. I hoped he screwed her lots and lots.

I patted Miranda's head, "It's okay. This will all make sense eventually. As for Jay, if he wants Victoria, he can have her. I'll talk to him about it. He is probably as bored with me as I am with him."

"See, you don't even care. I wish I didn't care. But I do Pagan. I care so much."

Of course, she did. If he was still Wyatt, I'd go slap him around and get the facts from him. It was weird to think the same soul, the same being was now someone else. Someone I didn't know all that well. I couldn't get away with slapping Nathan around.

"I'm going to get a shower, then will you go shopping with me? I need shoe therapy."

Dank was here. I remembered. I did not want to go shoe shopping. I wanted to go sit in Dank's lap for all of eternity. Well, and kiss him and do other things.

"Um, I guess, but I have somewhere I need to be later. Is this going to be an all day thing?"

Miranda raised and eyebrow at me, "What is it exactly that you need to do later?"

I could lie, but I'd probably get caught. I decided I'd go with the truth. "I'm seeing Dank Walker again. The whole thing with the girl didn't happen. It was another guy. I didn't hear things properly."

That was the truth.

Both Miranda's eyebrows shot up. "You're seeing Dank Walker again? Is he back? I haven't seen him in weeks. I figured he dropped out and traveled with the band."

I shifted my eyes around the room wondering where exactly he was. "Yep, he's back. Not traveling. Back…" I trailed off.

Miranda looked at me strangely. "Okay. Well, I'm going to get ready and you can wake up properly so that you can start actually making sense, and then we'll go buy shoes."

Once Miranda closed the bathroom door, I fell back on the bed. Crap. I did not want to go buy shoes.

Dank's body covered mine and his lips brushed my ear. "I'll go work. You have fun. But tonight, you're mine. We are going to go out and have fun. I want to take you dancing and hold you the way I wanted to that night at the club. Just promise me you'll wear those tan boots." Dank's voice was low as he spoke softly in my ear. I trembled and slid one of my legs up his hip.

"M'kay. That sounds nice."

Dank kissed a spot on my neck while his hand reached down and ran up the leg that I'd almost wrapped around his waist. "Miranda is going to be out soon. I need to go. Don't start something we can't finish."

I giggled and lowered my leg. "Okay, fine."

"I love you, Pagan," he said against my lips before he was gone.

Chapter Twenty-Four

Pagan

I waited outside the coffee shop at an umbrella table for Jay to arrive. I figured if I laid it all out there and gave him an out with me, then that would be settled. The Deity had screwed up with this soul mate match. If Jay didn't want me and I didn't want Jay, then there was no problem.

Dank was somewhere across the street watching me. He agreed that this might just work. Especially, if Jay is sleeping with another girl. But Dank wanted to be close by and, honestly, I felt like I'd just got him back after a very long separation. I didn't want him to go anywhere.

"Hey, Pagan. You already ordered. I'd have gotten your coffee," Jay said as he pulled out the chair across from me.

"I was in need of caffeine," I replied.

"I missed you at the frat house last night. It isn't any fun when you don't come with me."

I sat my cup down and looked him dead in the eyes. "Jay, I know that you have plenty of fun when I'm not there. I also know that you have all this fun while in bed or wherever you so choose to do it with Victoria. It's okay. I'm not mad. I just want us to lay it all out there and reach some form of closure."

Jay sat there with a stunned look on his face. Did the guy really think I wouldn't find out?

"I don't want closure. I want you. Yeah, so I might have messed around with Victoria some, but that is because you won't ever come to anything ATO has. I'm the only guy there without a date. Victoria is all over me. After a few drinks, it's hard to turn down."

I'm sure somewhere in all that he had a point. I just wasn't interested in it. "Our wants and needs are very different. You need things I can't give you or that I don't want to give you. It's perfectly okay that you need them. Getting them from Victoria is fine with me. But I just don't want to pretend like we have a relationship when you are having sex with someone else. We don't have a relationship. If someone else asks me out and I want to go, I will go."

Jay frowned, "Who asked you out?"

"That is beside the point. What this is about is the fact you have some sort of feelings for Victoria because I find it hard to believe you can just have sex with her over and over and feel nothing for her."

Jay put both his elbows on the table and buried his head in his hands. "I don't know what is wrong with me. I do want you, Pagan. I do. But she throws herself at me and I can't seem to turn her down."

Poor guy, he was clueless.

I reached over and patted his hand, "It's okay. You want her, she wants you. It is all okay. Just enjoy being free to be together. No reason to hide it from me."

Jay lifted his head and looked at me. "You've never been normal. Most girls would be pouring coffee over my head and screaming at me. You just pat my hand and tell me my sexual activities are okay. To go enjoy."

I laughed and stood up. "You were the one who wanted to pursue something between the two of us. Not me. I was never in this for anything resembling love. If I had been, then yes, I'd be devastated. But I just like you as a friend, Jay. I want you to be happy."

Jay leaned back in his chair. "This means I don't get another chance, doesn't it?"

Was he kidding me? I shook my head, "Nope, I'd say you're all out of chances. That ship has sailed."

"Can we still be friends?"

I glanced across the street and saw Dank leaning against a tree. His arms were crossed over his chest as he watched us closely. I knew he heard every word. "We can be friends from afar. No hanging out, just waving at each other in passing."

"I'll never forgive myself for losing you," Jay said.

"I'm thinking that you'll get over it. There is someone out there for you. Someone who won't bore you and loves the same things you do."

He shook his head, "It sure isn't Victoria."

I kind of disagreed with him, but I didn't say anything.

"Goodbye, Jay," I said for the last time, then turned and headed across the street. Dank was waiting for me on the other side. His smile made everything perfect. Knowing he was there and would always be there made everything okay.

I stepped out into the street with my eyes on him. The blaring horn and Dank's terror-filled eyes were the only warning I had.

* * * *

"No, Pagan. Don't you dare come out of there. You stay in there. Don't you leave your body."

I stared up at Dank, who looked frantic. His eyes were filled with unshed tears.

"Why are you so upset?"

"*No!* I said not to leave your body. Pagan, get back in there," Dank begged.

"She left it because she had to, Dankmar. Get a grip and think this through. You're Death, chill the fuck down." Gee's voice surprised me. It had an angelic ring to it that I'd never heard before. It was almost funny to hear her curse.

"Would one of you tell me why you're so upset?"

Sirens began to wail and I spun around to see an ambulance headed our way. Police sirens joined in and suddenly we were surrounded by a swarm of people. Two paramedics rushed toward me and bent down at my feet. How odd.

I looked down and saw myself laying there…oh, my God.

"Dank?" I asked, panicking as I watched a man pumping my chest and breathing into my mouth.

Two warm arms came around me. "It's okay, Pagan. We will figure this out. I will figure this out. This was not supposed to happen. You were not on the books. I would have known."

I wasn't on the books?

"Dank, am I dead?"

He didn't reply right away. "Gee, distract the paramedics and police. Distract everyone. I'm taking the body."

"You're what?" Gee asked incredulously.

"I said to distract them, dammit. I'm taking her body. Something is wrong. This was not supposed to happen."

Gee nodded and ran out into the crowd screaming, "Help me, please help me." Police officers started chasing her and both paramedics looked back to see what the commotion was. She was dodging the police and yelling at the paramedics that she needed mouth to mouth. She was having an allergic reaction.

I turned to look over at Dank as he was picking up my lifeless body. He grabbed my hand and we were no longer outside. We were walking through a dark drafty tunnel that was continuously spinning. I was too busy trying to figure out what was happening to think to ask Dank where we were.

Then we were walking out of the tunnel into my dorm room.

Dank laid my body down on the bed gently, as if it mattered. I wasn't in there anymore.

"Okay. You have to get back in there," he said looking back at me.

"Um, I don't know how," I replied. What was the big deal?

Dank walked over to me and grabbed my hands. His were cooler to the touch now. "Pagan, listen to me. If your soul is taken up, then you will be given another life. You won't be this age again for eighteen more years. I would have to wait until you matured to even approach you. Then there is the chance you will tell me to go away. We've already been through that. Please, baby, please. Don't leave me.

"She can't get back into the body, Dankmar," a deep smooth voice filled the room making the walls shake.

Dank pushed me behind him and turned to face the voice. "This was a mistake. She wasn't on the books. If you took her before her time, then a rule was broken."

Dank's body was strung tight as a bow. He was ready to fight whoever was in here. The fact their voice shook the room wasn't a comforting thought.

"We told you she had to choose" the voice said.

"She did choose," Dank shouted.

I raised my hand and peeked around the corner, a tall man at least eight feet tall since his head was grazing the ceiling gazed back at me with silver eyes. Completely silver—there were no pupils. "I did choose," I squeaked out. He was bigger than I'd thought.

"We are aware of her choice, Dankmar. We are also aware of *other things* as well."

I felt my face and neck heat up. So, they knew about…was there no privacy? I decided hiding behind Dank wasn't such a bad idea. I moved back out of the giant's sight.

"I didn't force her to choose. She never wanted him." Dank said with a defensive tone. He really needed to stop goading this man. Dank was big, but he wasn't *that* big.

"We are very capable of determining things ourselves. Now, if you would let me finish a complete thought before interrupting me, Death, that would be most appreciated."

Dank stood up straighter and reached back to put his hand in mine. I squeezed tightly, reassuring him I was here. No one had taken off with me. Yet.

"Have you considered the fact that she is a mortal? Her body will grow old and die. Were you planning on refusing to take her soul when her body is so old it can no longer function?"

"You promised me if she chose me, I could keep her for all eternity."

"Yes, we did and you shall. But there is only one way," there was a pause and then, "come here, Pagan."

Dank held my hand firmly and pulled me around to stand beside him. He didn't let go of my hand. "What do you want with her? What are you going to do?"

The man stared down at me and then raised his right hand into the air. A thick mist filled the room and the sound of rushing water roared in my ears. I squeezed Dank's hand tighter. A warm tingle began in my fingers and slowly spread throughout my soul. It wasn't unpleasant, but it was different. Something was happening. A loud crack caused me to jump and Dank's arms came around me.

"It is done. You've fought hard for her, Dankmar. We believe you chose well. Now, heed these words. She will live as long as you walk the earth. Your eternity will be hers. She will walk everywhere you walk. Her being is no longer that of soul or body. She is as you are, a form of deity. She may appear in any form. She is your mate. Her soul is no longer. It has been transformed. She will abide by the rules set in place. She may live this lifetime near those souls she loves. They will never know she has changed. They cannot. Her appearance to the humans she keeps close will change as they change. Once she is ready to walk away from the life she now leads she can let go of those rules and walk as you do without care."

I didn't understand most of what he'd just said. Looking up at Dank, I watched him nod. 'Thank you."

A swift breeze came through and then he was gone. I looked back at the bed—my body was gone, too.

Dank

"I'm gone or, at least, my body is gone," Pagan said in a hushed whisper.

Yes, her human body was gone. She would no longer need it. "Did you understand what he just said?"

Pagan began to nod her head, then she shook it and shrugged, "Maybe a little."

I laughed and bent down to kiss her forehead. "You will appear as I do. Miranda is about to walk through that door in a panic looking for you. She will see you. Nothing about you looks different to her. Only I can tell that you are no longer human. "

"So, I'm like you now?"

The door swung open and Miranda came running in and stopped dead in her tracks when she saw Pagan. "Pagan! You're alive. You're here. Thank God. Jay said you'd been hit by a car and that the paramedics came and then there was this commotion and then you were gone. Everyone is looking for you. We have to let them know you're alive." Miranda choked on a sob and threw her arms around Pagan. "I couldn't lose you too. I lost Wyatt, I can't lose you too."

My eyes met Pagan's over Miranda's shoulder and a smile tilted up the corners of her lips. We'd done it. Pagan didn't have to give up her life and I didn't have to give up Pagan.

"You won't ever lose me. I can promise you that," Pagan replied and winked at me before pulling back and squeezing Miranda's shoulders. "It's okay. I don't remember walking back here, but I did. Dank found me. I think I may possibly have had a concussion, but I'm fine now. Really."

Miranda nodded and kissed her cheek, "I love you, Pagan."

Pagan laughed, "I love you, too.

CHAPTER TWENTY-FIVE

Pagan

The security guard at tonight's club led me back to the room where Dank was waiting for me. The whole just-appearing-in-places thing was a lesson that Dank had yet to teach me. I always panicked at the last minute and ended up random places like service station restrooms or the milk aisle of grocery stores. I was providing Dank with endless entertainment with all my trials and errors.

The guard stopped in front of a door marked private and knocked once, then opened the door and stepped aside to let me enter. The room was similar to most of the rooms provided for him by the venues where Cold Soul played. There was a bar with drinks and bottles of water, and large sofas and chairs for seating. The walls of this one were lined with mirrors.

Dank was reclining on the couch, but he stood and walked over to me as the man closed the door behind me. "What took you so long?" he asked with a grin on his perfect face.

"Miranda and Nathan had a make up session in our room and I wasn't going anywhere near it until the noise stopped. "

"Ah, can't say I blame you. We really need to teach you how to change clothes at will. The only time I take off my clothes is with you. The rest of the time I just decide what I want to wear and my appearance changes."

I thought about that and decided I'd leave that lesson for later. My skills weren't great and the thought that I could end up naked in public because I'd done something wrong terrified me. "Let's not teach me that just yet."

Dank chuckled as if he had read my mind and knew exactly what my fear was. "You just let me know when you're ready. We'll work on it."

I nodded and he reached for my hand, pulling me over to the sofa. "I wrote a new song. After we, uh—" he looked over at me and a shy smile played on his lips.

"After we had sex?" I asked.

Dank shook his head, "No, Pagan, that was making love. Don't confuse the two."

Pleasure from his words coursed through me. I liked that this new body still felt sensations.

"I wrote it the morning after we made love. I haven't shared it with the band yet, because it's personal."

I sat down and he reached over and picked up the guitar lying on the chair beside me. He rested his foot on the edge of the sofa and slipped the guitar strap around his neck. Just when I thought Dank Walker couldn't get any sexier, he proved me wrong.

"What are you grinning about?" he asked looking down at me.

"Oh, I'm just thinking that I have the sexiest boyfriend on the planet. The only thing that could make this even better is if you were shirtless."

Dank smirked and pulled the guitar strap back over his head, then reached for the hem of his shirt and pulled it off tossing it in my lap. "This better?" he asked as he put the strap back around his neck.

"Oh my, yes."

Dank shook his head and laughed, "You make it hard on a guy, Pagan Moore. I was getting ready to be romantic and now my mind is all about the naughty."

I leaned back and crossed my legs and held his discarded shirt up to my nose to smell it. I may not give it back.

"Damn," Dank whispered as he watched me. "I don't think I remember the words to the song now."

I stuck out my bottom lip in a pout, "But I want to hear it."

Dank closed his eyes and adjusted his guitar on his bent knee. "Your wish is my command," he replied with a grin and then closed his eyes. His tongue darted out and licked his lips. Suddenly, hearing the song wasn't that important anymore. I wanted to lick his lips too. Then he began to play. I lifted my eyes from his lips as he opened his mouth. Our eyes met and he held me completely as his words joined the music.

"Daylight fades away as I watch you from a distance.
Darkness claims the sky and I wish you could only know.
We're supposed to be miles away, but something draws me closer.
We're supposed to be far away, but gravity brings us closer.

Closer than your skin, rebellion deep within, you've taken over me and I can't seem to swim to the top of myself. I'm under your control.

Wondering how we got here, wondering how we got here to the place we should go.

Oh-oh oh-oh, yeah
The place we should go.
Oh-oh-oh-oh
Oh-oh-oh-oh, yeah
Souls aren't meant for things like this.
Our worlds were never meant to collide.
You're better off leaving while you have something to leave behind.
We're supposed to be miles away, but something draws me closer.
We're supposed to be far away, but gravity brings us closer.
Closer than your skin, rebellion deep within.
You've taken over me and I can't seem to swim.
To the top of myself I'm under your control.
Wondering how we got here.

Wondering how we got here to the place we should go. We're supposed to be far away, but something draws me closer."

The moment his hands stopped moving, I was up and reaching for his guitar. I needed to hold him. Now. Dank understood my intentions and he slipped the guitar off and laid it down without taking his eyes off me. I hurled myself into his arms and grabbed his face, licking his lips before slipping my tongue into his mouth.

Dank's hand cupped my butt and he picked me up and I wrapped my legs around his waist. I loved him. He was mine.

"They're at it again. Damn, Dank gets more action than I do these days." Loose's voice interrupted us. Stupid drummer.

"Go away," Dank replied without looking back at our intruder.

"Can't, man. We go on in five," Les replied. Great, we had the entire band as an audience. I glared at them over Dank's shoulder, which only caused them all to laugh.

"Sorry we're breaking up your happy time, sweetheart, but we need our singer," Loose winked. He would have never winked if Dank's back had not been turned.

Rubber slapped him on the back of the head and murmured, "Dickhead."

Dank let me slide down his body, but kept his hands firmly on my backside. "I think I'm going to give this hobby up. You're the only audience I want. And these idiots keep messing with my free time."

I looked back at the three guys that made up most of the band. They had a keyboard player, Jet, who barely managed to show up right before the band went onto the stage. He was incredibly high all the time.

"They need you and I will always be waiting on the side of the stage when you're finished. Don't give this up because of me."

Dank tucked some hair behind my ear, "As long as you're waiting for me, I guess I can keep this up a while longer."

"Three minutes," Loose announced, reminding us they were still there.

I pressed my lips to Dank's, and gave him one fast kiss and then pushed him toward the door. "Let's go do this thing."

Dank

"When are you going to start letting Pagan come with?" Gee asked as we stepped into the hospital.

"I'm not. She may be immortal, but asking her to deal with this isn't something I will ever do." Death wasn't easy. It was a tragic thing to humans. Unlike me, Pagan had been human. She understood those emotions; she still experienced them. These emotions were a part of her. As much as I hated being away from her, I didn't want to bring her into this world.

"She is tough, Dankmar. The girl was able to force her memories to return through her heart. Her memories had been wiped clean, yet she brought them back and lived through it. Give her some credit."

I knew Pagan was tough. She loved me. Loving Death wasn't something that just anyone could do. I wasn't the bearer of good news.

"Leave this alone, please. I want to collect these souls and get back before Pagan and Miranda are done with their girls' night out."

"Well, I want to get back before Loose ends up banging some random slut in a bathroom stall. We all want something."

She was still seeing Loose. That was all kinds of screwed up. I didn't even want to consider what that might lead to. Gee was just a transporter. She wasn't a deity. She didn't have the power I did to get away with breaking rules.

"This still a fling, Gee?" I asked as we stood outside a hospital room where sobbing and heartache awaited us.

"I like his dreads, okay? And all that practice he's had screwing around has made him rather skillful in the area. He's just for fun."

She didn't sound convincing. This wasn't good. I'd deal with that later. Maybe Loose would end up ending this and I wouldn't have to handle it.

"It isn't like we see each other but a couple times a week. I know he is getting it elsewhere the rest of the week. I'm good with that. He's human, I'm not."

Nothing about her tone supported her statement that it was okay. She was going to go jealous-girlfriend on him really soon. God help the boy survive that. He'd never pissed off an immortal before. This could not be good.

* * * *

When I entered the room, I didn't see the soul I'd come to collect. However, the familiar face standing in the corner holding a weeping female caught my attention. Jay stood solemnly as he tightly held the blonde in his arms. I recognized her soul. It was the one he'd been unable to stay away from while he was dating Pagan. A translucent glow wrapped around their two bodies connecting their souls.

"Well, look what we have here," Gee said as she came up beside me, her attention captured by the visible bond between their souls.

"I didn't see this connection between them before," I said, studying them as Jay whispered soothing words in her ear.

The soul we'd come to collect walked away from the body on the bed. He was young. He was also trouble. There was a darkness surrounding him. The darkness marked him as hazardous. This soul wouldn't get another chance. He'd messed up in this lifetime.

"Uh, oh. We got a bad egg," Gee grumbled as I stepped forward to wrap the iron band reserved for angry souls around his wrist. It provided control for the transporter until she delivered the soul to its final resting place. Dealing with damaged souls could be tricky. Once I'd had to take them down myself, but over time, we figured out a better way to handle it. I didn't like wasting my time on the trip.

"Come on, bad boy. Let's get this over with," Gee told him.

This soul had been Victoria's mate. Now that it was damaged, the connection had transferred. Jay's soul was now complete.

CHAPTER 1
TWENTY-SIX

Pagan

My mom was peppering Dank with a million questions. It never occurred to me until Dank brought it up on our way here that when my memory had been taken away, so had my mom's. Dank had been wiped from the memory of everyone in my life. Miranda had forgotten about Dank and Leif just like I had. Although my memory was restored now, theirs were not. In doing so, it would completely mess with things. They'd know more than they should. My mom already had known more than she should. Now, Dank was the new guy I'd met at college. He was also the singer in a rock band.

Mom hadn't been pleased when I introduced him, but Dank and his charisma were quickly winning her over.

I brought him a glass of sweet tea before sinking down on the couch beside him. This was the way it was supposed to be. My mom would love him soon enough.

"So, you sing rock music? Do you do drugs?" my mom asked, watching his face for any sign of a lie.

I covered my mouth to keep from laughing.

"No, I don't take any drugs and I don't drink either. I never have. It's not something I'm interested in."

Mom nodded and cut her eyes to me. She was not impressed with my obvious amusement. "And you've been dating for how long? Because I thought you were seeing Jay again."

Dank tensed beside me and I patted his leg. "Jay is in love with a girl named Victoria. He thought he wanted to rekindle things with me, but it didn't work out. He and I don't go well together. We bored each other. It was during a brief time that Dank and I had a misunderstanding and I refused to talk to him."

Mom narrowed her eyes at me, "You do know to use protection, don't you?"

This time Dank had to cover his mouth with his fist to keep from laughing.

"*Mom!* Don't ask me things like that. I promise that *if* we were doing anything that required it, then, *yes*, we'd use protection."

My mother shrugged, "A mother can't be too careful. I needed to make sure you were thinking straight."

"I got this, mom," I assured her.

"Well, that's good. Now, tell me about this guy Miranda is seeing. I hear he is a sweetheart."

I reached over and grabbed Dank's hand and threaded my fingers through his. He had handled my mom's interrogation with flying colors.

"Well, I think it is very possible that Miranda may have found the one," I told her knowing good and well she had. Maybe not this year or the next, but one day, they'd end up married. In this lifetime and every one after it. Just knowing that I'd get to watch them find each other and fall in love in every life made me smile.

* * * *

Later that night, I was curled up in my bed. I hadn't realized how much I'd missed my room until I'd pulled my quilt over me and the smell of home hit me. I no longer required sleep, but I liked lying in bed at night.

Dank said it was something I'd trained myself to do and I shouldn't let go of anything that made me happy.

"This never gets old," Dank's voice said in the darkness.

I turned around to see him sitting in the chair he used to sit in to sing to me at night.

"What are you doing here?" I asked, sitting up. He was supposed to be out collecting souls.

"I'm about to go. I just couldn't resist coming in here and seeing you tucked into that bed one more time. I realized you owned me one night in this room. I was singing to you and you were sleeping. You made a little sound in your sleep like you were distressed and I panicked and ran to your side. You grabbed my arm in your sleep and pulled it up against your face and went back to sleep. I didn't want to ever move." He stood up and walked over to me. "I knew then that I had never understood what humans called love. But that if it was anything close to the power you held over me, then no wonder they searched for it so passionately."

I reached out and pulled him onto the bed with me. "You're going to be late," I told him as I pushed back the covers and reached for the hem of his shirt.

"Why?" Dank asked lifting his arms willingly so I could pull his shirt off.

"Because after hearing that, I can't let you leave until I've had my fill. Get naked, Dankmar."

The End

ABOUT THE AUTHOR

Abbi Glines is a #1 *New York Times, USA Today,* and *Wall Street Journal* bestselling author of the Rosemary Beach, Sea Breeze, Vincent Boys, and Existence series. She has a new YA series coming out in the fall of 2015 titled The Field Party Series. She never cooks unless baking during the Christmas holiday counts. She believes in ghosts and has a habit of asking people if their house is haunted before she goes in it. She drinks afternoon tea because she wants to be British but alas she was born in Alabama. When asked how many books she has written she has to stop and count on her fingers. When she's not locked away writing, she is reading, shopping (major shoe and purse addiction), sneaking off to the movies alone, and listening to the drama in her teenagers lives while making mental notes on the good stuff to use later. *Don't judge.*

You can connect with Abbi online in several different ways. She uses social media to procrastinate.

Facebook facebook.com/AbbiGlinesAuthor

Website AbbiGlines.com

Twitter https://twitter.com/AbbiGlines

Instagram: abbiglines

Snapchat: abbiglines

Printed in Germany
by Amazon Distribution
GmbH, Leipzig